Riverstone & Blood

By

Bradley Jones

Grosvenor House
Publishing Limited

This book is published by
Grosvenor House Publishing Ltd
Link House
140 The Broadway, Tolworth, Surrey, KT6 7HT.
www.grosvenorhousepublishing.co.uk

A CIP record for this book
is available from the British Library

Paperback ISBN 978-1-83615-148-7
Hardback ISBN 978-1-83615-149-4

Contents

Rivendale
Kilton
ARDENVIEL
Skell
Seacry
The Mines
Halcinde
Torreldane Woods
Hammerdeep
Blackhaven
Istana
Gorthak
N
W
E
S

Prologue

For thousands of years, the 5 races of Eldoria lived as one.

Skell, the mainland, was a sort of paradise, a beautiful place to live. Everyone coexisted in peace, no matter what race or house. There was little crime and no poverty. Everyone had food, water, and a roof above their head.

In the continent of Eldoria, lay different lands. Skell, which is considered the mainland, and then Blackhevan, Hammerdeep, Jotungard, Gruk'Thor, and Istana are all smaller islands surrounding Skell. The High King or Queen of Eldoria, ruler of them all

The High King, Draegon, ruled with an iron fist, along with the Royal Council, which was made up of people from all Five factions to show equality, he had created a dynasty where the elves, dwarfs, humans, orks, and snowpeople, who were half man half wolves, could co-exist and travel freely through the land with no fear or hostility. Punishment was handed out fiercely across the realm by the human King, who lived in the castle carved into the middle of Mount Morvem, located centrally in the capital city of Ardenviel. Somehow, the citizens loved the harsh punishments. Which outsiders felt was quite odd. Many people who travelled to Skell from afar were almost certainly baffled by the love, loyalty, and respect the people showed the King for such harshness. Of course, the small minority who didn't want to follow the rules hated the royal family and felt the punishments were far too extreme. The King didn't care about his critiques; he had created a safe haven, a place where decency and respect were the minimum; the people were just too scared of the punishments to risk committing crimes; in fact, many people who had committed crimes ran away to the arctic north or took their own lives, anything to escape the Island of Istana.

Any lawbreakers were sent on a one-way, ten-day journey to the desolate island of Istana, where survival seemed more like a cruel punishment than a test of endurance. This island was not just isolated from the rest of the world, but it was a place where hope came to die under the blistering sun amidst a wasteland of scorching sand, jagged rocks, and an unforgiving landscape that was home to many savage creatures. Sabre-tooth tigers, King cobras, venomous spiders, dragites... It was a prison of nature itself, and those unfortunate enough to be sent there were never heard from again. The prisoners who did survive made weapons and hunting gear and built tree houses to keep off the floor; the houses were never really big enough to do anything but sleep in them, but at least they were somewhat safe whilst they slept.

The constant presence of these predators created a suffocating sense of doom. Istana wasn't a place of rehabilitation or reform. It was a slow death sentence. Every dawn on the island was another fight for survival. The prisoners were left to fend for themselves, battling not only the unforgiving environment and deadly creatures but also each other. With no means of escape and only limited supplies, it became a brutal, desperate existence. Alliances were formed and broken; men and women turned on each other for scraps of food or drops of water. There were no rules in Istana—just the law of survival. The island was a place of exile, a place where lawbreakers were not sent to pay for their crimes but to simply disappear. It was a punishment that erased you from the world. The desert island was a prison that required no walls—its natural defences were far more terrifying than any chain or bar.

The thought of the horrors lurking around the coastline kept the prisoners on the Island; as bad as it was inland, at least they had a small chance of survival. In the surrounding waters, the Stomatosuchus patiently waited for prey. These beasts of the sea were known as the "sea demons." These monstrous, prehistoric predators were an unimaginable terror to anyone foolish enough to go further than knee-deep in the water. Fully grown, these creatures could reach lengths of ten meters, weighing around 1.5 tonnes, with their long, flattened skulls and lid-like jaws lined with conical teeth, capable of holding their prey with a vice-like grip. Their skulls alone stretched nearly two meters in length, making them seem even more monstrous when they surfaced.

There had been no war for 1000 summers, and the crown had always been in good hands, with each heir to the throne desperate to carry on the good work of their fathers and grandfathers. The thought of being 'that' King or queen to undo centuries of peace was enough to make the rulers work night and day to make sure things were right. Nobody wants to go down in the history books for the wrong reasons. Unfortunately, the generations of hard work were about to be unravelled, and the world was about to change....

Chapter One

"Lyle! Lyyylee!....Lyleeee, come here, Lyle!" Elaena's voice loudly echoed through the dense, shadowy expanse of Torreldane Woods as she called out for her young pup. She stepped carefully over a twisted root, her eyes darting between the thick trees and overgrown brush that surrounded her. Every so often, she'd hear a rustling in the distance, and hope would surge in her chest, only to be replaced by a creeping unease when it turned out to be nothing. "Lyle!" she called again, louder this time. The dog had been gone for over an hour now, chasing after a family of rabbits that had darted across the path during their afternoon walk. She had tried to catch him, but Lyle was fast, his golden coat flashing between the trees before disappearing completely into the distant shadows.

"Lyle! Lyle, come back!" Elaena shouted, holding back tears. The woods had grown darker than she'd expected, and the light was fading faster than it should have as she went deeper into the woods, the dense clumps of leaves floating in the sky, clinging onto the endless amounts of branches of the trees as they bounced up and down whilst the wind wrestled them continuously.

"Where are you, boy?" she whispered under her breath, pulling her silk silver cloak tighter around her small, quivering frame.

A gentle breeze stirred the leaves, and the tall grass around her swayed gently. From somewhere far off, she heard the faint splash of the nearby river. She followed the sound, thinking maybe Lyle had wandered towards the water for a drink. She ventured on; the ground became softer underfoot, the earth damp and cold. She wasn't sure how much further she should go before giving up.

She wouldn't give up, though; she couldn't. The thought of her little pup Lyle out in the woods all alone at night was enough motivation to keep her going; he was barely over a year old, and besides, he couldn't look after himself in the wild. He was so beautifully innocent, much like herself.

A flicker of movement caught her eye, and her heart leapt. She rushed towards it, her breath coming in short, sharp gasps. "Lyle! Is that you?"

As she reached the spot, she found only a pair of rabbits darting across her path, their fur glinting in the fading light. Maybe they were the rabbits he had been chasing? Does that mean he's close? She stood still for a moment, watching them disappear into the shadows. She was losing hope.

Elaena's heart pounded as she moved deeper into the thick woods, her breath coming in short, ragged gasps. She pressed on, forcing herself to focus on sound, ignoring the growing fear inside her. Every step took her further into the unknown, the familiar forest she had walked so many times now feeling strange and unwelcoming.

"Lyle, where are you, boy?" she called again, her voice cracking with both fear and hope.

Suddenly, a distant whimper emerged, and with every step, the sound became louder and closer. It sent a spark of relief through her chest.

"Lyle!" she shouted, her pace quickening.

Elaena stumbled over a fallen log, catching herself just before falling, and hurried towards the sound. Her heart raced, the urgency in Lyle's cries spurring her forward. She parted a curtain of hanging vines and found herself standing at the edge of a small clearing. There, half-hidden beneath a cluster of brambles and brush, was Lyle.

The golden retriever was tangled in the thick undergrowth, his fur matted with mud and twigs. His confused, wide brown eyes looked up at her. He whimpered softly, trying to free himself but only getting more ensnared in the vines.

"Oh, Lyle," Elaena said with a huge sigh of relief as she rushed to his side. She dropped to her knees and gently stroked his head, her hands shaking. "I've got you, boy. It's okay."

Lyle let out a small bark, wagging his tail weakly as she began to untangle him from the thorny brambles. The vines were tightly wrapped around his legs, and his fur was caught in the thick branches, but Elaena worked quickly, ignoring the scratches that the thorns left on her arms. As she pulled him free, she noticed a deep scratch along his side, likely from his frantic attempt to escape the undergrowth.

"There, almost done," she murmured, her voice soft and soothing. She gave the final tug, and Lyle was free.

Elaena held Lyle close as she gave a huge sigh. For hours, she had been dreading the moment she might have to return home without him. The idea of facing her parents, standing there with empty hands and tear-filled eyes, explaining that she had lost their beloved pup, was something she had been trying to push from her mind.

How could I ever tell them? she had thought, panic rising in her chest earlier when Lyle had first darted off after the rabbits. Her parents had trusted her to take Lyle for the walk alone—her first time being responsible for him. They had warned her about letting him off the leash, but she had always prided herself on how well-trained he was and how much he listened to her. That trust felt shattered when he bolted.

She had imagined their faces: her mother's disappointment, her father's worry. It wasn't just a dog to them—Lyle was like a part of the family. They've had him since birth, a rambunctious puppy who quickly wriggled his way into their hearts. Her father had spent hours training him, teaching him to fetch, sit, and stay. Losing him wouldn't just mean losing a pet; it would be like losing a promise they had made as a family.

A smile tugged at her lips as she pictured herself walking through the front door, Lyle wagging his tail at her heels. Her mother would fuss over the mud and scratches, scolding her gently for letting him run off. Her father, though—he would give her a knowing smile, maybe tousle her hair, and say something like, "That's why you never give up, El. You always keep going; the toughest people keep going when others would have given up." He'd always told her that, a lesson she now understood more than ever.

He immediately leapt into her arms, licking her face frantically as if to thank her for finding him. Elaena laughed through the tears of relief that had sprung to her eyes, hugging him close. His warmth was comforting, grounding her in the moment, reminding her that they were safe—for now.

Elaena Fikshire, a small elven girl, no more than ten summers old, knew she shouldn't have been alone whilst she was wandering the thick woodland. Now that she had found Lyle, she knew it was time to return home; she was shaken from the experience of losing Lyle; she now needed the comforts of home. Her shoulders dropped as she eased up, and the woodlands looked a little brighter than before. Now, she was relaxed, and it was almost as if her surroundings had become instantaneously more beautiful.

Now over the moon with joy, she danced along the Redmarch River, her laughter mingling with the songs of birds and the soft murmur of water rushing past. She had no notion of the destiny awaiting her just beyond the stream.

The young girl darted through the dense underbrush, her footsteps light and swift, barely disturbing the forest floor as she ran beside the winding river. The air was crisp, filled with the earthy scent of damp moss and pine, and the cool breeze carried the taste of adventure. As she ran, the girl could hear the whisper of the river to her right, its clear waters bubbling over smooth stones, weaving its path through the ancient forest like a thread of silver. Every now and then, a fish would leap from the surface, its scales flashing briefly in the sunlight before splashing back into the depths. The sound of the water mingled with the rustling leaves overhead, a symphony of nature that seemed to guide her forward.

She paused for a moment, catching her breath as she knelt by the riverbank, her fingertips brushing the cool, damp soil. Just beyond her, two squirrels chased each other up the trunk of a nearby oak, their tiny claws scratching against the bark. Their bushy tails flicked playfully as they spiralled upward, dodging branches and darting from tree to tree. She smiled, her heart lightened by their carefree antics.

She stood again, her eyes scanning the landscape ahead, long wet grass brushing against her legs as she moved. The world around her felt untamed yet peaceful, as if it had existed for centuries untouched by human hands. The river, ever constant, seemed to beckon her forward, inviting her to explore further into the unknown, but she knew adventure could wait; the warm walls of home were calling her. With a glance back at the chasing squirrels, now disappearing into the treetops, she grinned and skipped off again, her laughter mixing with the joyful barks from Lyle, her spirit as free as the creatures that lived around her.

Her eyes, keen as all elves' were, caught a glimpse of something strange—a glimmer, a flicker of light that did not belong to the dappled sunlight playing on the surface of the water. Curious, she waded across, her bare feet slipping briefly on the smooth stones beneath the water's surface. And there, half-buried in the soft mud on the riverbank, she saw a glowing stone.

At first glance, it seemed unremarkable, almost like an illusion. The stone held an otherworldly glow—a pale violet shimmer that drew her in. When she lifted it in her small hands, its warmth pulsed against her skin. And then, in an instant, the glow disappeared. The stone was dull and lifeless in her hands. Just a regular rock, but the sensation it left behind—not just heat—it felt like she was on fire, a rhythm of flames dancing in between her flesh and skin, like the heartbeat of something ancient and powerful.

Her pulse quickened, and the air around her felt different, charged. The vibrant green of the forest seemed sharper, more vivid. The river's hum turned into a symphony. Everything around her was alive in a way she had never felt before. She looked down at her hands—slender fingers now stained with the colour of the stone, her skin tingling with its power. Her reflection in the water, once that of a playful girl with soft auburn curls, now stared back at her with wide purple eyes and hair turned a shimmering white.

Panic gripped her for a moment, but deep inside, something else stirred.

Magic....It began small at first—little bursts of energy, flickers of light when she touched things. Leaves would fall from trees when she passed by; a pebble would lift from the ground with a mere thought.

As Elaena and Lyle made their way back home, walking at a slow pace, the child-like urge to run flooded her body.

"Come on, boy, let's go." The pair immediately started sprinting. She felt it instantly—a lightness in her step, the feeling of the wind rushing past her face in a way it never had before. The dense woods, once a puzzle of trees, flowers, and paths, now seemed easier to navigate. Every step felt surer, swifter, as if the very ground beneath her feet propelled her forward. She'd never moved so fast, not even on horseback.

She glanced back at Lyle, expecting him to be bounding along beside her as he always did. But to her surprise, he was lagging behind, his little legs working hard to keep pace. His usual energetic strides seemed laboured now, his tongue lolling out of his mouth as he tried to catch up.

"Lyle, come on!" Elaena called, her voice carrying over the rustling leaves. She slowed down for a moment, giving him a chance to close the distance between them. But as soon as she picked up her pace again, it became clear that something was different. She was moving faster than she ever had before, faster than she should have been able to.

Her heart raced, her skin almost tearing apart from the heaps of energy now within her. She darted around a large oak tree with ease, her feet barely touching the ground as she manoeuvred through the forest like a swift breeze. The familiar path home seemed to blur beneath her as her legs carried her effortlessly over rocks and roots that would have normally slowed her down.

What is happening to me? she thought, her mind reeling as the world around her seemed to stretch and contract with each step. It wasn't just speed—it was something more. She could feel the energy surging through her, a pulse of power that made everything feel sharper, more alive. Her senses were heightened—the rustle of the leaves, the distant gurgle of the stream, and even the sound of Lyle's paws hitting the dirt seemed amplified in her ears.

She glanced down at her hands, her fingers still tingling from the strange energy she had felt when she touched the glowing stone by the river. Could this be the stone's doing? Was this new speed part of the magic that had awakened inside her?

She slowed down again, looking back at Lyle with concern. The poor pup was panting heavily, his legs moving furiously as he struggled to keep up. Guilt washed over her, and she quickly bent down, calling him over. He wagged his tail weakly, grateful for the chance to rest as he trotted up to her side, licking her hand in thanks.

"Sorry, boy," she murmured, stroking his head softly. "I don't know what's happening; I'm not used to waiting for you!"

Elaena stood there for a moment, catching her breath. She could feel it now—an undeniable shift inside her. Her body was different. Faster, stronger. The world itself seemed different, too. It was as though the magic she had stumbled upon had begun to seep into every part of her being, altering her in ways she hadn't fully grasped yet.

The walk back to her house seemed longer than usual. Every shadow in the woods seemed to stretch, every tree more imposing. The stone, now tucked safely in the pouch at her side, felt heavier with each step. Elaena's eyes kept drifting back to it, recalling the pulse of energy that had coursed through her body when she first touched it. The word 'magic' felt strange in her mind, but she couldn't deny what she had seen—what she had felt. That brief moment where the world around her seemed more alive, more vibrant, filled with possibilities beyond her understanding.

The hills began to flatten. She could see the stone walls of Ardenviel, where within those walls, her little family home waited for them both.

Elaena approached the towering stone walls of the city, Lyle trotting beside her; she felt a surge of worry. The gates were open, and the city folk were bustling about their day—merchants unloading carts, children chasing each other through the streets, and guards watching over everything with sharp eyes. She pulled up the hood of her cloak, trying to hide her newly transformed hair and eyes, her heart racing as they passed under the massive stone archway.

She kept her head down as she moved through the busy streets, avoiding eye contact with the people around her. The last thing she needed was for someone to notice the strange, shimmering white of her hair or the glowing purple of her eyes.

With every step she took, she felt the weight of their gazes, as if, at any moment, someone would stop her and ask what had happened. Lyle stayed close to her side, his golden coat drawing a few admiring glances, but no one seemed to notice the change in Elaena. She quickened her pace, the familiar streets of the city passing in a blur as she focused on reaching home.

When they neared her house, the familiar stone walls and arched doorway coming into view, she let out a quiet breath of relief. Soon, she would be safe behind closed doors, where she could figure out what had happened to her without prying eyes.

Her father was there, leaning against the architrave of the doorway, smoking a pipe with his arms crossed as if he had been expecting her. When Elaena reached him, her words stumbled out. "I—Lyle ran off... I found him near the river, and there was this—" She stopped herself, unsure how to explain the glowing stone, unsure if she even should.

"Elaena..." he whispered, stepping closer, his hand gently tilting her chin upward to meet his eyes. He studied her face as he painted a picture. His thumb lightly brushed across her cheek as if to confirm that what he was seeing wasn't some trick of the fading light.

"Your eyes..." he murmured, barely audible.

She blinked, confused at his words. His tone was different, as if Lyle running off didn't matter.

"Wh—why are they different?" he continued to stutter.

"There was this—"

"Quick, get inside," her father quickly interrupted whilst dragging her in by the shoulder.

He stepped back, still staring at her intently. Her once warm, hazel eyes had shifted—now, they shimmered with a strange, faint purple hue, a deep violet that seemed to swirl beneath the surface. They were no longer the eyes of the child he had known. It was subtle but unmistakable, the glow barely visible in the dim light but enough to unsettle him.

"And your hair..." His hand reached out to touch a lock of it, his fingers brushing the strands with disbelief. The soft auburn curls she had inherited from her mother now shimmered like silver in the moonlight, streaks of iridescent white woven through them like threads of starlight.

"Where did you go, and what happened? Tell it now and tell it true," her father Braegon demanded.

Her eyes widened as he spoke, the weight of his words sinking in. "Well, I was just walking with Lyle, and he ran away after a few rabbits. I found him near a river in Torreldane woods, and then I saw a stone shining brighter than the sun; it was in the water, so I picked it up, and suddenly I was different?"

Her father was shaken. "So you just picked up a rock, and now you have purple eyes and silver hair; what do you take me for, Elaena? A fool?"

"I am telling you the truth, don't believe me, I don't care!"

"Do you forget your place in this house, girl? Watch your tongue!" exclaimed Braegon. "Now stop with the tales and tell me how you traded the colour of your eyes!"

"It was the stone!" Elaena screamed aggressively, reaching into her pocket and pulling out the stone; she then threw it in rage to her left.

Braegon froze, his eyes wide as he watched the stone smash through the wall, leaving a gaping hole in the solid stone that had once seemed impenetrable. Dust and fragments of rock crumbled to the floor, the sound of the impact still echoing through the house. He stood there, staring at the destruction in disbelief, his mouth hanging slightly open as his mind raced to process what had just happened.

Elaena, breathing heavily from the outburst, stood motionless, her hands trembling. The moment felt surreal, as if time itself had slowed down. She glanced from the hole in the wall back to her father, her purple eyes shimmering with a mix of fear and defiance.

Braegon's gaze shifted from the ruined wall to his daughter, his expression now one of dawning realisation. For a moment, there was only silence, broken by the faint creaking of the wooden beams above. The air between them felt charged, thick with the weight of what had just occurred.

"You're telling the truth..." he whispered, the disbelief in his voice giving way to something else—something darker. His eyes narrowed, and a twisted smile tugged at the corners of his mouth. "It's real."

Elaena took a step back, uneasy at the sudden change in his demeanour. She had never seen her father look at her this way before—like she was something more than just his daughter. Something valuable. Something powerful.

He moved closer, his gaze fixed on her with an intensity that sent a shiver down her spine. "The stone...you've consumed its power; it has made you powerful, different."

"You can't tell anyone, Elaena; we need to keep this to ourselves until we figure things out. When your mother comes back from the market, we will explain what has just happened."

Braegon's mind raced, a torrent of thoughts and visions swirling as the reality of what had just happened sank in. The stone—the magic—was real. And his daughter, Elaena, was at the centre of it. His grip tightened on her shoulders as his mind spun with the implications, the possibilities. The impossible had just become possible, and with that realisation came a flood of ambition he had never before dared to entertain.

He saw it now, as clearly as if it were unfolding before him: a future where they wielded unimaginable power. The King now seemed weak and complacent, sitting on his throne in the heart of the Kingdom, surrounded by his council of fools. This would make him the ultimate traitor as he was part of the royal council himself, but he had always secretly despised them all. Braegon's hands itched at the thought of it. With this power, he could crush the old order and tear down the stagnant system that had kept men like him in the shadows, scraping by whilst the royal family bathed in luxury.

His mind raced further, each thought sharper and more intoxicating than the last. *With Elaena's magic...no one could stand in our way.* He saw the nobles bowing before him, their faces pale with fear and awe. The guards, the King's loyal enforcers, would be useless against such raw, untapped power. The very walls of the King's castle would crumble as easily as the one in their home had.

And he would be there, standing at Elaena's side—not as a father, but as a ruler. The Elves would chant his name, sing of their rise, their strength. They would rewrite the history books, his name etched beside hers, as the ones who toppled the ancient order.

His eyes gleamed; the vivid images of his future now felt so tantalisingly realistic. He envisioned it all—crowns, banners, armies marching under his command. The lands of Skell bending to his will, the people kneeling in fear and reverence. The King's head on a spike. And at the heart of it all: Elaena, his daughter, the vessel of the magic that would make it all possible.

What else could this power do? Braegon's thoughts raced faster. Could she bend others to her will? Summon storms? Level cities? The vision gripped him, intoxicating, unstoppable.

Her father's voice lowered: "The next few years will be important, Elaena. You have to stay hidden. Stay safe. We'll train, we'll prepare, and when the time is right, we'll uncover the full extent of what you can do. But for now, we wait. We'll use the quiet. We'll make sure no one knows."

Elaena nodded, feeling the gravity of his words settle over her like a weight. There were so many questions swirling in her mind—about the stone, about her power, about what he father was thinking. But for now, she simply took comfort in the fact that she wouldn't have to face it alone. Her father would be there, guiding her, preparing her for whatever was to come.

Power, magic, destiny—all of it lay before her, waiting. She just had to be ready.

Chapter Two

Days passed by, and people started to ask questions about Elaena's strange new appearance. Rumours spread widely across the city. Her father, Braegon, was growing impatient. As Elaena grew, so did the force within her. Braegon had always been ambitious, driven by visions of the elven race claiming its rightful place at the top of the hierarchy of Skell. In his eyes, High King Draegon's rule was a human legacy, an accident of history that needed correction. And now, with his daughter, the first wielder of magic in all of Eldoria, he saw the chance to make his dreams a reality.

The scheming began in secret, and so the 'Firm' was born.

At first, whispers of the 'Firm' spread quietly among trusted elven allies—a secretive and ambitious group formed by Braegon. He was determined to see his race ascend to dominance in the Kingdom of Skell. Braegon, deeply discontented with the reign of High King Draegon, believed that the human-dominated rule was a mistake of history that needed to be overturned. The Firm was born from his vision of an elven resurgence. Braegon's voice constantly manipulated Elaena's impressionable young ears as her growing powers drew others to their cause. The plan was simple yet diabolical: undermine the royal family by spreading lies and using when the time was right, strike fast and hard using magic to tip the scales in their favour and overthrow the King; nobody would stand in the way of their dreams.

Eight summers later, Elaena, the first wielder of magic in Eldoria, possessed now immense power.

The time had come; Elaena was a young adult; she was no longer a naive child; she was an intelligent and extremely powerful young elven mage. Her arsenal was one to fear; she had spent years studying herself with other scientists, constantly pushing her body to the limit every day.

She could manipulate the elements of mother nature to her will, summoning fire, controlling water, commanding the wind, or shaping the earth. She could conjure illusions to deceive or hide from enemies, making herself or others invisible or altering the appearance of landscapes. Elaena could also read minds, influencing thoughts or emotions to control and manipulate those around her; she could slow the ageing of herself and her father or anyone she wanted. Telekinesis would allow her to move objects without touching them, whilst the power of foresight could give her glimpses of possible futures, helping her and the Firm navigate their plans. With the power of enchantment, she could infuse objects with magical properties, creating weapons or tools imbued with magical abilities. It was frightening.

Almost 500 members of the Firm had sworn loyalty to Braegon Fikshire, some of whom loved their new leader and shared his ideology, and others who were terrified of being on the wrong side of Elaena. They knew she was unstoppable.

Eventually, the Elves decided the day had come. That night, they would unleash hell.

The night had finally come. Braegon Fikshire, leader of the Firm and mastermind of the elven rebellion, led his 500-strong army of traitorous elves through the streets of Skell's capital, their faces hidden beneath dark hoods, their ragged armour clinking with each step. This army, a mix of the devoted and the fearful, marched in grim silence, gripping their swords with might, knowing that the night would forever alter the fate of Eldoria. At the head of the procession strode Elaena, no longer the impressionable child but a fully grown mage of terrifying power. Flames flickered in her clenched fists, her aura like an untamed storm as she waved her arms with purpose, casting her magic upon the screaming townsfolk who were once her neighbours.

Without hesitation, Elaena unleashed her wrath. The city, once proud and bustling, became a warzone as fire bombs exploded against walls, setting homes ablaze. Lightning bolts rained down from the heavens, incinerating soldiers where they stood into a pile of bone dust. Ice spikes erupted from the earth, splitting the helpless souls of the unfortunate in half. Her power spared no one—soldiers, guards, civilians, and even entire buildings fell victim to her fury. Braegon watched from behind, satisfied as chaos spread like wildfire. His dream of an elven resurgence was finally in motion. He gave a slight smile, with a look of evil in his eyes, as his daughter turned to look at him from a distance. He was proud; his daughter was leading the charge in a war against the rule of High King Draegon, and his flesh and blood were leading the elves to a glorious and historic victory.

The elves moved through the streets, ruthless in their assault, leaving devastation in their wake. Civilians fled in terror, only to find their paths blocked by the hooded devils who showed no mercy. Buildings crumbled under the weight of Elaena's magic, and the once-great capital of Skell was reduced to smouldering ruins. The Firm's strike was as precise as it was brutal, with Elaena's immense magical abilities tipping the scales in their favour, just as Braegon had always planned.

With each step forward, the elves claimed more ground, their dominance cemented by the destruction that Elaena wrought. The city of Skell was all but destroyed, and the echoes of death and violence reverberated across Eldoria. In a matter of hours, Braegon's rebellion halved the population of the realm, marking one of the darkest chapters in its history.

Thousands upon thousands lay dead in the street, a massacre of the masses; it was like sheep to a slaughterhouse. Yet for elves, it was the beginning of a new era—they would reign supreme, with the only mage in the universe at their side.

After laying waste to the capital, Braegon and his elven army of traitors set their sights on Heavnskeep, the towering castle perched high above the city. The path leading up the mountain was long and treacherous, winding through steep cliffs and sharp turns, but the elves marched relentlessly. With Elaena at the front, her magic clearing any obstacles, they reached the towering gates at the foot of the mountain. The gates, meant to protect the castle from invaders, were no match for the elves' sheer force. They broke through with ease, pushing their way up the stone steps that led to the castle's entrance, every step bringing them closer to their ultimate goal.

At this point, any opposition forces were fleeing for their lives; Elaena and her soldiers had stopped attacking, showing mercy to the ones who were unfortunate enough to live to tell the tales.

At the top, they reached the castle's main hall, where the High King Draegon awaited with his family, surrounded by 200 trembling knights of Ardenviel. The knights, once the pride of the Kingdom, now stood frozen in fear, knowing that the elven army they faced was unlike anything they had ever encountered. The elven mage approached the giant steel doors calmly, walking slowly, almost dramatically, as if she knew she was indestructible. She placed her hands alongside the middle of the twinned steel doors and flexed her fingers. The two mammoth-like doors flew backwards into the hall, piercing through the anxiety, floating like bubbles in the atmosphere, squashing a handful of the King's defenders. She then stopped and scanned the room before slowly raising her arms. The humans just looked in shock and horror, frozen in time as they each knew it was the last moment on this earth. As she raised her arms, the swords were ripped out of the human soldier's pathetic little hands and lifted slowly into the air. As she slowly rotated her skinny and fragile womanly wrists, the swords of the doomed knights slowly rotated until the sharp end pointed directly towards every one of them. Suddenly, she bowed with a burst of speed, her arms now down by her side, bowing almost as if she had finished the performance of a lifetime. The swords ripped through the skulls of the men; brains and blood exploded everywhere as they collapsed one by one. She killed them all instantly. The last hope of the royal family was slain at that moment, leaving only Draegon and his terrified family in the hall, cowering in the back like a group of infants crying after a scolding.

Braegon stepped forward, a look of cold satisfaction on his face as he approached the King, who was surrounded by the corpses of his bloodied knights, already buried by the warm bodies of their fallen brethren. The King looked into the eyes of the man who had orchestrated this bloodshed, tears running down his face. Braegon's voice was calm, filled with a chilling certainty. "This Kingdom was never meant to be yours, Draegon," he said, his tone devoid of mercy. "Your rule is over. The elves will take their rightful place, and your bloodline ends tonight."

The King, defiant but powerless, exchanged final words of protest, "Why Braegon?" he cried.

Braegon stared blankley, before asking: "Is this how you want to be remembered? In your final minutes? Whimpering like a woman!" Braegon chuckled.

Without hesitation, the former council member drew his sword, and with one swift strike, he ended Draegon's life. His blade gleamed with the blood of the King as Braegon turned his attention to the queen and the children as they screamed. One by one, he cut them down, their cries echoing through the empty hall. In a matter of moments, the royal family of Skell was no more.

As Braegon stood over the bodies, his victory complete, he knew that the throne of Skell now belonged to the elves. The rebellion was over, and a new era had begun, with him and his daughter, Elaena, standing as the architects of a brutal, historic conquest.

That night, approximately 80,000 were murdered across all five factions, the city was destroyed, and wildlife surrounding the city was destroyed.

The chilling sound of murder and violence spread like wildfire in the air, burning through the night as the population of all living things in Skell was halved in a night. Mass devastation swept across the realm of Eldoria; it was the darkest time in the land's history.

Soon after the victory, Braegon Fikshire claimed the throne for himself; he had the power of his daughter behind him and the respect of all the elves for leading them to victory. Braegon used his new position to banish the four factions from the mainland forever.

The Humans and Dwarves, forced to flee east, left the mainland with wariness in their hearts, both keeping a watchful eye on each other as they scrambled for safety. The humans, slightly ahead, sailed towards Blackhaven, a fortified island to the east, leaving the Dwarves no choice but to navigate further north to the rugged island of Hammerdeep, several miles from Blackhaven. There, they began to rebuild, separated by the cold waters but ever mindful of their human neighbours.

The Snowpeople, meanwhile, retreated north, relentlessly pursued by elven forces for days. Their attempts to settle along the way were futile—first in Kilton, then Rivendale—each time driven out by the elves' pursuit. Finally, with no choice left, they fled to the northern shoreline. Fortune favoured them as the sea was frozen solid, and they made a desperate, slippery dash across to the distant, arctic isle of Jotungard, where they found refuge at last.

To the south, the Orks embarked on a slow, arduous journey, winding their way through treacherous mountain passes and the ash-filled lands of volcanoes—the home of the fire giants. Unlike the Snowpeople, the Orks needed no chasing. They had no desire to linger near the capital, where it was too dangerous, and they were not welcome anyhow. Nor did they wish to head north to the freezing lands of ice and snow. The Orks had never taken to the cold, and the prospect of battling relentless winters held no appeal. The Orks, though battle-hardened and fierce, were eager for a fresh start as they made their way towards Gruk'Thor, which was the most southern island and was always at a nice toasty temperature. The thought of staying in Skell, the land that had seen too much bloodshed and betrayal, filled them with unease. Skell had been tainted by war, its soil soaked with the memories of fallen kin and enemies alike. It was no place for rebuilding, no place for peace. They craved a land where they could raise their young without fear, a place where their traditions could thrive, far from the watchful eyes of their enemies. The warmth of Gruk'Thor promised that sanctuary. It would be their new stronghold, a land where the Orks could flourish once more and put Skell—and its bitter memories—far behind them.

Weeks passed, and more and more survivors joined their friends and family away from Skell. The dispersal of the four rival factions sparked an idea in the new High King's twisted and power-hungry, pea-sized brain. He decided to use Elaena to cast a magic spell over Skell, which made it invisible to outsiders. They couldn't see it, and they couldn't touch it; it just simply disappeared. High King Braegon Fikshire was now infamously known as 'Braegon the Banisher' by many across the land.

Skell's banished races were left in a whirlwind of confusion, grief, and seething anger after they realised they could never return to their homeland. This banishment was a crushing blow. It wasn't just the loss of their homes; it was the loss of their identity. The lands they had fought for, lived on, and loved were ripped away from them forever. The brutal massacre had halved the population, leaving the survivors with deep scars, not only in their hearts but in the very fabric of their being. Eldoria had seen its darkest hour, and there was no turning back.

One hundred twenty years passed since the land of Skell vanished. The elves thrived unchallenged and were rich in materials, castles, weaponry, food, and land. On the other Islands, housing the four other races, new generations were bred, and the people who lived through the great betrayal of the High King Draegon had naturally passed away. All four factions had rebuilt their communities in their new territories, and the once war-tarnished lands of Skell had regrown as beautiful as ever. All relationships between each Island and race were non-existent, and hatred was prevalent. Each nation was extremely intolerable and hostile towards the other.

After a long reign of power, the High King died at age 177, and he was replaced by his son Zelder.

Just a few weeks after the passing of the late High King, Elaena died from old age; the magic could only prolong the lives of herself and her family, not save them from death, and at the grand age of 141, she took her last breath. The cruel banishing spell was lifted upon her death, and the mainland was no longer hidden from the other four factions. After 120 summers of rule, Elaena Fikshire passed from the world, and with her death, the magic that had hidden Skell began to fade. The island reappeared like a shadow at dawn, visible once more to the eyes of those who had been exiled.

Zelder, the newly crowned King of the Elves, stood at the precipice of overwhelming responsibility. His father, Braegon Fikshire, had passed away, leaving him the throne of Skell, a burden of heavy expectations. The death of his father was only one of the weights Zelder bore on his shoulders. The recent passing of Elaena, his beloved sister, whose magical power had been both a beacon of strength and the glue holding together the elven Kingdom, left a deep, emotional scar on Zelder.

The time of reckoning was near, and Zelder was thrown in at the deep end. Skell was no longer hidden or safe; the tides of history, once still, began to stir again.

Chapter Three

The bells of Ardenviel rang out across the land, their deep, mournful toll echoing through the once-great city.

Elaena Fikshire lay in her coffin, as her brother Zelder wept besides it, "I'm going to miss you so much, sister; you have left us with everything; history will not forget who you are. You are the saviour of the elves. I love you so much."

Her once luminous white hair, now returning to its darker natural form, framed her delicate features, her skin pale as moonlight, her closed eyes concealing the fierce violet glow they once held. Though her body had stilled, an aura of grace and majesty still clung to her, as if the very air around her refused to forget the power she had once wielded. She looked more like a sleeping goddess than a fallen queen, her peaceful expression carrying the weight of a thousand untold stories.

The coffin that held her was a masterpiece of elven craftsmanship, woven from the richest materials the earth had to offer. Its base was crafted from diamonds so pure they sparkled like starlight, catching the soft glow of the enchanted lanterns that surrounded her. The surface was smooth, the flawless facets of the diamonds glistening in the twilight, reflecting rainbows of light in the sombre space. Gold and silver filigree traced along the edges, intertwined in intricate patterns that resembled the ancient elven runes of protection and peace, each detail meticulously carved by the finest elven artisans. Precious stones—sapphires, emeralds, and amethysts—adorned the sides, adding splashes of deep, vibrant colour to the otherwise ethereal structure.

The lid, a transparent crystalline case, was equally mesmerising. It shimmered faintly with the last echoes of Elaena's magic, making it appear as though the very air within her tomb had become enchanted. Every curve and angle of the coffin was a testament to the love and respect her people had for her. The craftsmanship was unparalleled, the finest hands in all of Skell having laboured over it for days, ensuring that their queen's final resting place was worthy of her legacy.

As she lay there, dressed in flowing robes of silver and violet, the colours of her house, Elaena looked like a vision from another universe, her body wrapped in the beauty and power of the world she had once ruled. Though her death had left a hollow void in the hearts of her people, the sight of her resting in this masterwork of earth's rarest treasures was both heart-wrenching and breathtaking. The silence of the thousands gathered to witness the passing of their queen was deafening. She was the most powerful being ever to walk the lands of Eldoria, though, in the hearts of many, her death signalled something more than the loss of a God. It felt like the end of an era for the elves. Elaena was never actually the Queen of Skell; the throne went directly to her brother, the heir to the throne, Zelder. The people of Skell called her the queen, as the word princess didn't seem significant enough for the women they worshipped. It didn't truly represent the way they felt about her.

Above the city, the sky flickered strangely. The phenomenon had begun days before her death—an unnatural shimmering, like the fabric of the heavens themselves, was unraveling. It started when Elaena first showed signs of weakness, it was subtle: brief moments where the air would ripple as though disturbed by a gust of wind unseen. But as the days passed, the flickering grew more intense, a ghostly light appearing and disappearing, as if something in the sun itself was beginning to fade.

The grand courtyard of Ardenviel, once a place of laughter and light, was now draped in sombre silence. Purple and silver banners fluttered gently in the soft breeze, their once-vibrant hues muted by the clouded sky.

King Zelder Fikshire stood over his sister's body, his features cold and unreadable. He was a tall, imposing figure with sharp, elven features and a gaze that carried both pride and ambition. He had none of his sister's magic, and despite all the wealth and power the elves had gained during their 120 years of rule, he knew their dominion over Skell was fading, just like the sky above.

The funeral lasted through the day and into the twilight hours. The elves chanted ancient hymns, songs of sorrow and memory, as their queen was laid to rest in a tomb beneath the great oak of Ardenviel. But as the last words of the rites were spoken, something far more profound began to happen.

Far beyond the borders of Skell, on the islands where the banished factions had lived in exile for more than a century, the sky had been flickering for days as well. The snowpeople in the frozen wastelands of Jotungard had gazed at the heavens with unease. The Dwarves of Hammerdeep had seen the stars themselves seem to blink out of existence for moments at a time. And on the Orkish island of Gruk'Thor, warriors had watched with suspicion as the horizon shimmered like a mirage.

For years, the mainland of Skell had been nothing more than a myth to those in exile. Hidden from their view by Elaena's magic, it was as though the world had swallowed it whole, leaving nothing behind but a vast, empty ocean. The lands they had once called home were now invisible, lost behind an impenetrable veil of sorcery. But as the days wore on and the flickering in the sky grew more intense, something changed.

On the night of Elaena's funeral, when the last light of day slipped below the horizon and darkness covered the land, the sky itself seemed to tear open.

Skell's stability crumbled before the young king's eyes. With Elaena's death, the magical spell that cloaked the mainland from outsiders had vanished. For the first time in 120 years, the other four factions could see Skell again, a land they had once called home. The world King Zelder inherited was no longer a peaceful one but rather a realm ready to explode into violent vengeance.

Zelder had always been close to Elaena, although their relationship had been complex. Elaena was adored by the elves but feared by others. She had been instrumental in shaping the political landscape of Skell, and though she wielded great power, she was deeply private, hiding her insecurities beneath a composed exterior. Zelder had often looked to her as a mentor and protector, someone who shielded the Kingdom from chaos. Now, with her gone, he felt unmoored, as if a part of his foundation had crumbled.

The transition to becoming King was testing. The coronation ceremony, a beautiful spectacle, was held in the grand halls of Ardenviel Castle; unfortunately, though, it was void of the usual joy that accompanied such occasions. The newly crowned King wore the ceremonial robes, the weight of the crown feeling heavier than it should have. The elves gathered to witness the event, but there was little celebration, no cheering. It was a moment marked more by grief and uncertainty than triumph. The King could smell it in the air; he could see it in the empty glares of his subjects; the people didn't want him on the throne; after all, he had been thrust into the role without any knowledge.

As King Zelder took the throne, he couldn't shake the feeling that he was not ready; he questioned his ability to lead. How could he rule a Kingdom that was now exposed to its enemies? How could he ensure the safety of his people when the very foundation of their protection—the magic was gone? The threat of the other factions, now aware that Skell was no longer hidden, loomed on the horizon. Would they seek revenge for the banishment, or would they attempt to reclaim the land that was once theirs?

Zelder often visited the royal crypt, where both Braegon and Elaena were entombed. He would sit in silence, contemplating the choices they had made and the consequences that had followed. In these quiet moments, he realised that whilst he could not bring back the dead, he could learn from their legacies. His father had built an empire on power and fear, but perhaps it was time to rebuild Skell on something else. The hatred between the factions could not continue forever; it would only lead to more destruction and more death. Elaena, in her final years, had hinted at the possibility of reconciliation, though she never acted on it. Now, Zelder had the opportunity to change the course of history, to heal the wounds that had festered for over a century.

He could feel the growing unrest among the Elves, many of whom believed that the other factions would soon seek to explore the shores of the newly visible island. Suddenly, it seemed everyone had a plan of action, and the only person left without one was the King himself. The gossiping was relentless, every handmaiden in every manor. Every butcher on every corner of the market. Every farmer, blacksmith, and diplomate. Every mother, child, cat, and dog. It was becoming an invisible noose around the King's scimpish neck; he just wanted the world to swallow him up. Some urged him to take preemptive action, to strike before the other factions could organise an attack. Others, more cautious, seeking peace, suggesting that the banishment had lasted long enough and that it was time to reunite the realm. Zelder was torn. His father had ruled with an iron fist, maintaining the division between the factions with force. Elaena had been the key to sustaining that division with her magic. Without them, he had to chart his own path forward.

Zelder often found himself deep in thought; he would repeatedly play the same ideas and images in his head, a future where the five factions of Eldoria could once again live in peace. The path to that future was unclear, and the threat of war still hung in the air, but he was determined to find a way to lead his people through the darkness, even if it meant confronting the very legacy his father had left behind.

After many sleepless nights, Zelder sat on his throne, plucking grapes from a silver bowl, lost in thought. His patience was wearing thin. He sighed deeply and finally made a decision. “Fetch Elandril,” he ordered a young handmaiden.

“Yes, Your Grace,” she replied, scurrying away.

Moments later, Elandril entered the room, humming softly to himself as he glided through the door. His cloak swayed gently with each step, his body moving to the rhythm of his quiet song. “Your Majesty,” Elandril greeted, bowing with a smile.

“What puts you in such high spirits, Elandril? Do I look cheerful?” Zelder asked, his face giving the obvious answer..

Elandril straightened up, locking eyes with the King. A smirk slowly spread across his face. “Forgive me, Your Grace, but this is the first time since your crowning that you’ve summoned me. Your grief has settled, and you are ready to face important matters. That alone is cause for good spirits.”

A heavy silence settled in the grand hall. Zelder suddenly slammed the silver bowl to the ground, sending grapes rolling in every direction. He stood abruptly and strode towards Elandril, his boots echoing with purpose. He stopped just as the tips of their shoes met, staring the older man dead in the eye before bursting into laughter. “You’ve always been an odd one, Elandril.” The king chuckled. “Come, walk with me to the Council chamber. It’s time we called a meeting. There are important matters to discuss.”

Elandril, still grinning, nodded and followed the King as they left the hall, their footsteps resonating through the empty corridors as they prepared to face the uncertain future.

The Royal Council chamber in Ardenviel Castle was an impressive but cold room built deep into the mountain; the room was mainly made out of marble, gold, and obsidian, its tall windows letting in shafts of light from the in-door city that did little to warm the walls. The ancient tapestries of the elven Kingdom hung heavy with history, portraying victories and conquests, reminders of a legacy built on blood. Zelder sat at the head of the long, obsidian table, flanked by the members of his Royal Council. His face was stoic, but his mind churned with conflicting thoughts as he looked into the faces of those who had served his father for decades.

Each council member represented a pillar of the elven elite—military, diplomacy, economics, and magic. King Zelder opened the discussion, his voice calm, though an undercurrent of anxiety hummed beneath it. “As you all know, we are now visible to the world. The question is, when will outsiders visit our land? I believe our first course of action should be to seek dialogue—to offer peace and reparations. What my father did to them...was cruel. We can undo that. Perhaps there is still a way to restore balance to avoid war. I say we send a handful of knights paired with negotiators to sit and wait on the shores of Skell. The power of speech is greater than any.”

There was a pause in the room, the silence thick with tension. At the far end of the table, Laerion, the commander of the elven army, leaned forward, his sharp features hardening into a frown. “Your Majesty,” he began, his tone careful but firm, “I appreciate your optimism but fear you are underestimating the hatred the other factions have for us. What your father did was necessary for us; he ensured the survival and prosperity of the Elves. The Dwarves, the Orks, the Snowpeople—they won’t come seeking peace. They will come for revenge. If we approach them with weakness, we will see our horses return with the heads of the knights you speak of sending.”

Zelder shifted uncomfortably in his seat. “But we have the advantage, Laerion. We’ve had centuries to prepare whilst they’ve been scattered across their islands. We could extend a hand before a sword.”

Next to Laerion, Elandril, the council’s senior diplomat, nodded gravely. “Your Grace, the factions were not merely banished; they were butchered and humiliated, bled of their pride, torn from their homeland, and cast out like dogs. You speak of reparations—what could we offer them that would be enough to heal such wounds? They will not negotiate in good faith. Peace is a noble thought, but one that belongs to an era long past. They will not forget the injustices of the war. Plus, for the first time in a century, we are without Elaena to shield us; they will see our vulnerability.”

A heavy weight pressed down on Zelder's chest. He had always imagined himself as a different kind of King than his father—one who would bring peace and reconciliation to a land long divided. But now, confronted by the unwavering certainty of his council, he felt that vision slipping through his fingers. "Are we so sure that there is no room for forgiveness? That we cannot heal what was broken?" His voice was quieter now, betraying his doubt.

From across the table, Nioma, the council's magical advisor, spoke next. Nioma's position was always questioned; she had never had magic powers, obviously, but she spent hours studying Elaena; she had a great understanding of her power, but now she was dead....and many councillors didn't know why she was still there. Her silver hair shimmered in the light as she gazed at Zelder with something akin to pity. "Forgiveness requires the willingness of both parties, Your Majesty. And there is no willingness among those we wronged. They have spent generations teaching their children to hate us, to curse the name of Braegon the Banisher. We cannot erase that hatred with a simple offer of peace. The world outside our borders is not the one you hope it to be. It is far darker and far more dangerous."

Zelder kicked at the air beneath the table. Every word they spoke rang with cold truth, but it was a truth he did not want to accept. "So what, then?" he asked, his voice tinged with frustration. "Do we simply wait for them to come, and when they do, we meet them with steel? More bloodshed? More war? My father's legacy may have made us strong, but it also made us feared and hated."

Laerion straightened in his chair, his eyes narrowing. "Yes. War is the only language they will understand now. You say we have the advantage—we do, for now. But if we do not act decisively, if we do not prepare to defend ourselves, that advantage will slip away. The factions will not come as disorganised refugees; they will come as conquerors. You must be ready to defend the throne, to defend our people, by any means necessary."

Zelder's heart pounded in his chest. A cold sweat began to bead on his forehead. He had never wanted to be like his father, to rule through fear and force, but the weight of responsibility was pressing down on him with crushing intensity. His people looked to him for protection, and if the other factions truly sought revenge, then any attempt at peace could lead to the slaughter of his kin. Was he willing to risk that?

Elandril leaned forward, his voice softer now but no less firm. "Your Majesty, you are a just and thoughtful king, and that is admirable. But you cannot afford to be naive. The factions will see your desire for peace as weakness, and they will exploit it. You cannot undo your father's work—not without risking everything we have built. The time for peace has passed."

The words echoed in Zelder's mind, circling like vultures around his sinking hope. He felt a fire begin to ignite deep within him—a defensive instinct, a growing anger at the thought of his enemies setting foot on elven soil. His mind, once filled with dreams of reconciliation, was now clouded with fear and resentment. The idea of welcoming the factions back, of offering them any kindness, began to seem absurd. They would come to destroy, not to make peace. He had no choice but to defend his people.

Laerion saw the shift in Zelder's expression, the hardening of his gaze, and seized the moment. "We must be ready for war, Your Majesty. Strength is the only thing that will keep them at bay. Show them that we are still the rulers of Skell, that this land belongs to the elves and no one else. If they dare to land on our shores, we will meet them with the full force of our armies. We will make them regret ever thinking they could return."

Zelder nodded slowly, his decision settling into his bones like iron. The idealism that had once guided him was now fading, replaced by a cold determination to protect his kingdom at all costs. He rose from his seat, and the council followed, standing in deference to their king.

"It seems you have made my dreams seem nothing more than a fantasy, Laerion; I want to trust in your guidance. I know I'm young, and I think it would be foolish of me to ignore you. I want you to train all of our men, I want you to plan for any possibility, and I want you to have multiple plans of action; we need to be five steps ahead," Zelder said before sighing in defeat. "If they come, we will be ready. And we will destroy anyone who dares to set foot on elven land."

The council members bowed their heads in agreement, satisfied that their King had finally embraced the reality of the situation. But as Zelder left the chamber, the shadows of doubt lingered in his heart, now buried beneath a growing storm of anger and fear. He had once dreamed of peace, but now, his mind was fixed on war.

Hammer deep

In the Dwarven Kingdom of Hammerdeep, miners and artisans emerged from their deep caverns to witness the sight. The stars, which had been flickering for weeks, suddenly flared with a brilliant, unnatural light. The horizon rippled like water, and then, for the first time in over a century, they saw it: the distant outline of the mainland.

The Dwarven King, Tholgar Ironfist, stood atop the great battlements of Hammerdeep's fortress and watched in awe as the land of Skell reappeared on the horizon like a ghost from the past. His heart, which had hardened over years of exile, pounded with a mixture of hope and dread. The magic was gone. The mainland was visible once more.

Gruk'Thor

On Gruk'Thor, the Orks were less subtle. Great bonfires were lit, and the warriors of the Redaxe Clan howled with joy at the sight of their long-lost homeland. Their chieftain, Gron Ironfang, watched silently, his massive frame silhouetted against the flames. He had been a child when his people were banished, and now, with Skell's reappearance, the call for vengeance rose once more among his clansmen.

Jotungard

In the icy reaches of Jotungard, the snowpeople, with their glistening, thick fur and shimmering eyes, stood as still as statues, their breath visible in the freezing air. The eldest of their kind, High Priestess Ylvana, raised her hands to the heavens, her voice like the wind as she chanted ancient words. They knew, as the others did that the magic that had kept them at bay was gone, and soon, the land would be contested once more.

Blackhaven

Nestled on the human Island of Blackhaven, a young Princess named Marcella stood at the cliffs, staring in disbelief as the veil over Skell lifted. The once-mighty city, where her ancestors had ruled as Kings, now appeared like a distant shadow, beckoning. Her father, Lord Cael, gripped the hilt of his sword, his eyes narrowing as the distant mainland came into focus.

Skell

Back in Skell, the elven capital of Ardenviel trembled with unease. The flickering sky now burned with a faint purple glow—the last remnants of Elaena's magic as it dissipated into the ether. Zelder Fikshire stood at the balcony of the palace, his eyes scanning the distant horizon, where he knew the other factions were watching.

"The spell is broken," he muttered under his breath, his voice heavy with a mixture of fear and anger. The years of prosperity had made the elves strong, but without his sister's magic to protect them, no longer naive to the threat, he knew what was coming. War.

Skell had returned to the world, and with it came the inevitable wrath of the exiled factions, long nursing their wounds and grievances. The flickering sky was a warning, a sign that the peace once forged in blood and fire would soon be tested once more.

King Zelder turned and walked back into the palace, his mind already racing with plans for fortifications, alliances, and strategies. The elves would not surrender their throne so easily. But deep down, in the pit of his stomach, he felt the weight of destiny pressing down on him.

The era of Elaena was over, and a new chapter of Skell's history was about to begin—one that would be written in bloodshed.

Chapter Four

The mainland of Skell loomed on the horizon, its rugged silhouette finally breaking free from the magical veil that had shrouded it for over a century. The vibrant hues of the sky, once a kaleidoscope of flickering lights, had faded away, revealing a world now ripe with uncertainty, aspirations, and the stirring of long-dormant hopes.

On the islands surrounding Skell, the exiled factions, weary yet resolute, prepared for the first time in 120 years to reclaim the land that had once been their sanctuary. Tension hung thick in the air, each heart pounding with the weight of what might come next.

In the dimly lit war room of Blackhaven's citadel, tension hung thick in the air as King Cael Emberfall stood before his council.

King Cael Emberfall is a striking figure, even at the age of fifty. Standing at nearly six and a half feet tall, his presence alone commands attention. His strong, angular jawline and high cheekbones lend a regal dignity to his features, but it's his piercing, steel-grey eyes that hold the attention of anyone who dares meet his gaze. Those eyes, sharp and calculating, speak of a man who has seen the harsh realities of leadership and battle but has never let them diminish his sense of control.

Despite his age, Cael retains much of the handsomeness of his youth. His skin, though lightly weathered by the years, still holds a tanned warmth, a testament to his many days spent outdoors, overseeing the vast lands of his Kingdom. His dark brown hair is peppered with silver at the temples, cropped short, and neatly groomed, giving him a distinguished look that befits his royal status. His neatly trimmed beard mirrors the same touch of grey, accentuating the strong lines of his face.

King Cael wears light armour, a unique blend of practicality and elegance. His armour is made from fine, polished steel, designed not only for protection but to allow for quick movement. The chest plate is adorned with intricate engravings of flames and swords, symbolising the Emberfall lineage—a family known for both their strength in combat and their fiery will to rule. The armour, whilst functional, is sleek and close-fitting, highlighting his broad shoulders and lean, muscular build, honed from years of battle and training.

Attached to his armour is a cloak of deep crimson, the colour of blood and fire, a symbol of his Kingdom's power and his personal resolve. The fabric is of the highest quality, heavy enough to flow dramatically as he walks yet light enough not to impede his movements. The cloak is fastened with a silver clasp in the shape of a Yak, the Blackhaven native animal, adding a touch of belonging to his otherwise battle-ready appearance.

Around his waist, Cael wears a leather belt with a finely crafted sword sheathed at his side. The hilt is engraved with gold accents, a family heirloom passed down through generations of human Kings, though it is clear from the wear of the grip that this sword is not merely for show—it has been used in battle, and Cael is no stranger to wielding it.

Cael's posture is always upright, and his movements are deliberate, embodying both the grace of a royal and the strength of a warrior. He is a man who balances the responsibilities of rulership with the readiness for combat. Though his face remains stoic and composed, there is a flicker of fire behind his gaze, a passion that suggests he is not content to sit idle on the throne. He is a King who knows the weight of his crown but also revels in the power it brings, and there is no doubt in the minds of those around him that he will do whatever it takes to protect his people—and his legacy.

Stood next to Cael was his beautiful daughter, Princess Marcella Emberfall, a vision of ethereal beauty, embodying both grace and strength. She possesses long, flowing black hair that shimmers like a polished boot, framing her delicate face and accentuating her striking features. Her eyes, a mesmerising blend of emerald and silver, mirror her father's steely resolve yet hold a warmth and kindness that draws people to her, making her not just a royal figure but a symbol of nature's beauty.

They both stood waiting eagerly for the members of the council to arrive, as they usually do, very slowly. The massive table in the centre of the room bore an unfurled map of Eldoria. The map was a vital tool they possessed, and it was crucial to understanding the logistical problems they commonly faced whilst on their quests to better the lives of their Island.

Suddenly, the sky sort of exploded, a millisecond of blinding light; without hesitation, everyone dashed to the windows to catch a glimpse. Marcella wanted a closer look.

The princess rushed outside and pounced upon her well-trained, silver-coated giant Yak called Theo. She wasted no time getting comfy as she grabbed the long leather reins of the saddle and flicked them aggressively as she steered the now galloping Yak towards the coastline. She approached the end of the long wooden dock, her heart racing as she peered through her rusting binoculars, the cold metal pressing against her skin. The salty sea breeze tousled her hair, wrapping around her like a gentle whisper from the past, mingling with the distant sound of waves crashing against the dock's pillars. She could hear the rhythmic lap of the water, punctuated by the occasional call of a seagull soaring above, harmonising with her growing anticipation. Gazing into the distance, her breath hitched as she beheld Skell, the long-lost island that haunted her dreams.

Just a few miles away, it beckoned her with a promise of heritage and adventure. The sheer cliffs rose magnificently, their white faces gleaming in the sun, creating a stark contrast against the backdrop of a golden sandy beach that shimmered like tiny jewels. As she focused her binoculars, she could make out the lush, tropical trees swaying gently in a warm, inviting breeze behind the cliffs, their vibrant green leaves dancing in the sunlight. The scent of saltwater mixed with the sweet fragrance of nearby blooming flowers only exaggerated her imagination, and her thoughts ran away as she imagined what it would be like to go over there. The sight of the island filled her with giddiness, evoking memories of stories her grandmother told her about their ancestors who once roamed that very land. Every detail filled her with a sense of longing and excitement; she could almost feel the warmth of the sun on her skin and the thrill of adventure coursing through her veins.

King Cael called Marcella through the window, asking her to come back to the war room they had previously stood in, where the last of the council members had just joined him.

Marcella swiftly obeyed her father and joined him in the gloomy room. "The magic is gone," Marcella began, her voice steady despite the flicker of anxiety in her eyes. "But why? This island has been hidden for over a century. Why reveal itself now?" Her eyes squinting in concentration as she took in the map before her. King Cael came and stood next to her and crossed his arms, his gaze unwavering as it scanned the distant horizon. "Elaena must be dead. The spell was intricately tied to her life force. With her passing, the veil has lifted. I think from this point on, we should heavily focus our thoughts on putting my family back on the throne, as it's our birthright."

A murmur of concern rippled through the council.

"But what does this mean for us?" one member asked, his brow deeply furrowed. "The elves held dominion for so long. Are they weakened now, or are they merely biding their time to defend what's theirs? Is this some sort of trickery? A trap, perhaps?" His voice was thick with apprehension, reflecting a fear shared by many in the room.

King Cael leaned closer to the map, his finger tracing the southern shores of Skell. "We don't know yet," he replied, his tone grave. "That's why we can't afford to rush in blindly. We'll send a ship to scout the coastline. If the elves are still powerful, we'll need to consider forming alliances—perhaps with the dwarves or the snowpeople."

Marcella shook her head in disagreement, her hand instinctively resting on the hilt of her sword. "Why would either of those clans want to team with us? We have been enemies since the war; I wouldn't trust them." Marcella paused in thought, then continued, "And what about the Orks? Do you propose we try to befriend them too?"

King Cael's expression darkened. "The Orks will be the first to charge in, driven by their relentless thirst for blood. We must tread carefully. Let them make the initial move whilst we gather vital information." He paused, his gaze shifting to Marcella. "You'll lead the scouting party."

The council murmured with a mix of surprise and apprehension.

"Are we really prepared for this?" one of the elder members interjected, his voice tinged with worry. "We're at a disadvantage here—physically outmatched by the other species. The elves are agile, and the Orks are brutal. What if we're viewed as the weaker faction?"

"We can't let fear dictate our actions," King Cael countered, though his worry flickered in his eyes. "We humans may not possess their strength, but we have cunning and resolve. Marcella, you'll leave at first light. We'll approach the Eastern shores cautiously. If the elves are lying in wait, we'll know soon enough. We need to be strategic, and you need to go there and back unseen; we can't afford to give away that we have even noticed what's happened."

Marcella nodded quickly, a mix of determination and apprehension in her expression. "I'll prepare the team," she said firmly. "But we must remember:

if we're seen as weaker, we must play to our strengths. We can't let our physical disadvantage dictate our fate." King Cael loudly interrupts before Marcella can get another word out, "What has gotten into you all? Why are you all so fearful? We haven't even gotten there yet. Have you forgotten that we humans used to sit on the throne? How do you think our ancestors managed that? We have more advanced weaponry than they did; that is our advantage, and that is why we will succeed. Marcella, I don't feel confident in you leading. I don't think you're ready; you're not battle-hardened yet, my dear. You are ripe with fear; I will take the lead; it was unfair of me to put such pressure on your young shoulders."

As the council members exchanged glances, the gravity of their situation settled in. They were united not only by their fears but also by their resolve to face whatever lay ahead. The fate of Blackhaven—and perhaps the balance of power in Skell—depended on their next move.

Days passed as the good people of Blackhaven helped prepare the ship and crew for sail. Freshly forged Armour and weapons were gifted as a token of luck to the select few who were about to embark on the historical journey across the choppy tides of the sea.

Marcella stood outside the stables, her heart heavy with the weight of the decision she had made. She gazed at her loyal Theo, his eyes tired after she had just woken him from a long nap. The creature, towering and gentle, had been her companion through countless adventures, always by her side. But now, as she prepared to embark on a mission fraught with danger, she knew she couldn't take it with her.

Slowly, she walked over, her hand brushing along Theo's thick, velvety fur. The yak huffed softly, its large, soulful eyes meeting hers as if it sensed her inner turmoil. Marcella leaned into his warmth, wrapping her arms around his massive neck in a gentle embrace. "I wish you were coming with me," she whispered, her voice soft but edged with sorrow. "But it's too dangerous this time."

Theo nudged her shoulder, a gesture of comfort, as if understanding her words. Marcella pulled back and smiled sadly. She had always felt a unique bond with the creature, one that transcended words. She knew it would have followed her into battle without hesitation, but she couldn't bear the thought of putting him in harm's way.

Kneeling beside him, she ensured he had plenty of fresh water and a generous pile of hay for the coming days. "I've made sure you'll be taken care of," she continued, her voice trembling just slightly. "I'll be back before you know it. You just need to stay here and be safe. I promise I won't be gone long."

The yak let out a soft grunt, and Marcella chuckled through her growing sadness, pressing her forehead gently against the animal's snout. "You've always been there for me, haven't you? Love you, Theo," she said as she kissed him on his fluffy head.

She took a deep breath, standing up and brushing her hands against her leather belt. The sky was beginning to darken, signalling the start of her mission. Marcella patted the yak's side one last time before stepping back. "I'll see you soon, okay?"

Theo watched her as she walked away, its large eyes filled with a quiet, loyal understanding. Marcella didn't look back, not trusting herself to keep it together if she saw the creature's gaze again. With each step, she felt the tears accumulating, but she managed to hold them in as she made her way over to the docks, where men were working hard to prepare the ships to leave. She could remember the day she tamed him like it was yesterday.

Not everyone on the island of Blackhaven owned a yak; in fact, these magnificent creatures were reserved exclusively for the upper class—families with long, distinguished histories, the highborn. The citizens of Blackhaven could still interact with the wild yaks, of course. It wasn't uncommon to see people stroking their soft, thick fur, offering them treats like fruits from the tops of trees or other hard-to-reach places the yaks could never access on their own. But taming one? That was a different story entirely. Attempting to tame a yak without permission was considered a serious crime, and those caught doing so would face severe consequences.

Yaks were revered as prestigious animals, their majestic presence unmatched by any other creature in the realm. The humans of Blackhaven believed that no animal embodied the same level of grace, power, and loyalty as these big, round, soft-hearted beasts. But taming a yak wasn't easy, and it had to be done at a very specific point in the animal's life. Only between the ages of 24 and 30 months could a yak be successfully tamed—a discovery that had taken humans many years to understand.

Attempting to tame a yak any earlier would likely result in disaster. The mothers were fiercely protective of their calves, and trying to approach one too soon could easily lead to being trampled. As the yak grew older, however, the mother would gradually loosen her protective hold, allowing her offspring to become more independent, much like humans did with their children. The key was to tame the yak during the period when it was no longer fully reliant on its mother but still young enough to seek guidance, care, and affection.

This sweet spot, between 24 and 30 months, was when the yak was most open to bonding with a new master. If you waited too long and the yak became fully independent, it would be nearly impossible to form that connection—yaks were known for their stubborn nature. Some people considered the process of taming a yak to be selfish, arguing that it kept the animal in a perpetual state of dependency. But the truth was, a tamed yak lived a life of luxury. They were fed the finest delicacies the land had to offer, whereas their wild counterparts often went without, foraging for scraps in the wilderness, so as you can imagine, Theo was a lucky boy to be tamed by a Princess.

For the upper-class families of Blackhaven, owning a yak wasn't just a symbol of wealth; it was a tradition, a bond that reflected their privileged status and connection to the majestic creatures of the land.

Taming a yak was a delicate and patient process, requiring both trust and persistence. It wasn't simply a matter of grabbing the reins and asserting dominance. The bond between yak and master had to be nurtured gradually, with the understanding that these majestic creatures were sensitive, stubborn, and intelligent. The entire process typically spanned about a month, though it could sometimes take longer depending on the yak's temperament.

Week 1: Earning Trust

The first step in taming a yak was a careful and quiet approach. One had to be slow, deliberate, and non-threatening, usually with a gift of food in hand—delicious fruits that the yak could not easily access on its own, such as the papaya or mangosteen, which grew on trees very close to a sharp cliffs edge. Approaching a baby yak too quickly would spook it, and the bond might never form. It would also definitely trigger the mother to attack you.

The tamer would be wise to approach from the side, not head-on, as a frontal approach could be seen as a challenge by the observing mother. The yak's immense size meant it could easily become defensive if startled, so the key was patience. Holding the fruit at arm's length, the tamer would extend it just enough to allow the yak to sniff and consider the offering. The first few days were usually spent just letting the yak eat from the hand, getting it used to human presence without attempting to touch or control it.

The goal of the first week was simple: to let the yak associate the trainer with something positive—food. No sudden movements, no attempts at control, just a calm presence.

Week 2: Establishing Contact

Once the yak had grown accustomed to the human presence and accepted food without hesitation, the next step was to initiate gentle physical contact. This was a critical phase because it established a deeper level of trust between the yak and the tamer. Beginning with soft pats and strokes along the yak's massive shoulders and neck, the trainer had to move slowly and deliberately. Rushing this stage could result in the yak withdrawing or becoming aggressive.

Whilst offering the usual fruit, the trainer would slowly begin petting the yak's thick coat, starting in familiar spots where the yak was already comfortable.

Over time, the goal was to work up to more sensitive areas, like its head or face. The yak would need to grow accustomed to being handled, especially in places that might later be harnessed.

Throughout this second week, the trainer also introduced a soft rope—just to get the yak used to seeing it. The rope wasn't used yet, but it was important for the yak to associate it with the training process and not view it as a threat.

Week 3: Introducing the Rope and Basic Commands

By the third week, the yak should be comfortable with physical contact, and now was the time to begin introducing the rope in earnest. The rope was placed loosely around the yak's neck, not to restrain it but to help guide it and get the yak used to the sensation of light control.

This phase required constant reassurance. With one hand on the rope and another offering a treat, the trainer would gently coax the yak to take small steps forward or sideways. The rope wasn't used for pulling but for directing, with gentle tugs to guide the yak in the desired direction. Verbal commands or whistles were also introduced at this stage, allowing the yak to associate sound cues with movement.

At this stage, it was common for the yak to resist a bit—pulling back, stopping, or simply ignoring the commands. The tamer had to be persistent but calm, never using force but instead rewarding the yak with more fruit and kind words when it followed the cues. Establishing these basic commands took patience, and it was important to never lose temper, as yaks were quick to sense tension.

Week 4: Strengthening the Bond and Establishing Routine

By the fourth week, the yak had typically accepted its tamer as a trusted companion. Now, the focus was on routine and repetition, making sure the commands and physical guidance became second nature to the animal. More complex manoeuvres could be introduced, such as turning or stopping on command, and the rope was used more firmly, though never harshly.

The yak would also be introduced to saddles or light harnesses at this stage, getting it used to bearing weight or responding to more controlled commands with someone sitting on its wide, meaty back. This phase was crucial for ensuring that the yak didn't just tolerate human presence but genuinely accepted its tamer as a leader.

Daily walks became routine, with the yak learning to follow alongside the trainer without resistance. Rewards of food, water, and affection were still a regular part of the process, reinforcing the bond between the two. The yak learned that the human was its provider and protector, solidifying the connection.

Final Phase: Bonding for Life

By the end of the month, the yak and its trainer had formed a strong, trusting relationship. The yak had learned to respond to commands, follow gentle directions, and accept saddles or other equipment. More importantly, the bond between them was one of mutual love and respect. The yak saw its trainer not as a master but as a partner, someone who provided for its needs and ensured its well-being.

The tamer would now take the yak on longer walks and let it sleep in the stables outside one's home. You would also introduce it to group environments with other yaks, allowing the animal to understand its place within both human and yak society. From this point onward, the yak would be a loyal companion, ready to follow its master's commands and contribute to life on the island.

Although taming a yak required patience and care, those who succeeded gained not just an animal but a lifelong companion and a cool means of transport.

The last of the supply crates were loaded onto the ship, and it set sail from Blackhaven's harbour; the creaking of the wooden hull and the rhythmic crash of the waves against the bow filled the air. The small vessel, carrying King Cael, his daughter Marcella, and a select group of their finest warriors, cut through the choppy waters like a blade. The horizon stretched endlessly before them, a hazy line between the sky and sea that seemed to beckon with both promise and danger.

Marcella stood at the stern of the ship, her eyes fixed on the receding shores of the island that had been her home all her life. The sea breeze tugged at her dark hair, and the salt-laden air stung her cheeks. She'd never felt so far from solid ground before, and it unsettled her deeply.

With a quiet sigh, she made her way to the front of the boat, where her father, King Cael, stood gazing into the distant horizon. His posture was as resolute as ever, his broad frame silhouetted against the fading light of the evening sun. For a long moment, Marcella hesitated, unsure how to voice the turmoil swirling within her. Finally, she found her words.

"Dad," she began softly, her voice barely audible above the sound of the waves. "I don't blame you for thinking I'm not ready. The truth is, I'm not." She looked down, fidgeting with the hilt of her sword. "I'm terrified. I've never left the island before, and now...everything feels so uncertain. I just—" She faltered, her voice trembling. "I feel uneasy. What do you think is out there?"

King Cael turned to face his daughter, his expression softening as he saw the fear in her eyes. He placed a comforting hand on her shoulder, his touch firm but gentle. "Marcella," he said, his voice low and steady, "it's normal to feel afraid. You're not the only one on this ship with doubts. I'd wager that every man and woman here is carrying their own uncertainties, their own fears."

Marcella glanced up at him, searching his face for reassurance. "But you never seem afraid," she whispered.

A wry smile tugged at the corner of the King's lips. "That's because I've had years of practice hiding it," he replied. He turned back towards the sea, his eyes distant as if recalling a long-buried memory. "I remember my first battle at sea. I was about your age—young, brash, and full of fire. But when we set sail into unknown waters, I was absolutely petrified."

Marcella blinked in surprise. She had always imagined her father as the embodiment of strength and confidence, someone who never wavered in the face of danger. To hear him admit to fear was startling.

"I'll never forget the sight of the enemy ships on the horizon," Cael continued, his voice quieter now, almost lost to the wind. "It was the first time I had truly felt my own mortality. The battle was chaos—arrows flying, swords clashing, the roar of the waves louder than the roar of war." He paused, his hand tightening slightly on her shoulder. "I nearly died that day. An arrow grazed my side, and for a moment, I thought it was the end. But I survived, and with that experience came a lesson I've carried with me ever since."

Marcella was silent, her heart racing as she imagined her father, younger and less sure, fighting for his life on the open sea.

"The truth is," King Cael continued, "we can never be fully prepared for what's out there. But we learn. We grow stronger with every challenge we face. That fear you feel? It's a sign that you care—about your people, about our future. And that's not something to be ashamed of."

Marcella swallowed, her throat tight with emotion. "But what if I fail? What if I make a mistake?"

Her father's gaze softened, and he turned to face her fully, his hands resting on her shoulders now. "Then you'll learn from it, just like I did. Failure is not the end, Marcella. It's part of the journey. And no matter what happens, you won't be facing it alone." He smiled gently. "We're all in this together." Quickly nudging her with a serious tone, he added, "Unless the failure kills you. Then you'll be dead; hard to learn from that, isn't it? Haha," The King gently patted his daughter on the shoulder as he erupted with laughter.

Marcella's heart swelled with gratitude. Her father's words, simple as they were, lifted a weight off her chest. The uncertainty was still there, lurking in the back of her mind, but now it felt more manageable, less suffocating, and the light-hearted banter at the end did tickle her; she just didn't want to show it.

King Cael glanced towards the horizon once more, his expression calm but resolute. "As for what's out there," he said, "I don't know. But whatever it is, we'll face it head-on. We're Stormborns, after all. It's in our blood to weather the storm, no matter how fierce."

Marcella nodded, her resolve hardening. The fear was still there, but alongside it now was a growing sense of purpose. She wasn't alone in this. Her father was right—they would face whatever came their way together.

As the ship sailed deeper into the unknown, father and daughter stood side by side, gazing out into the distant horizon. The sea stretched endlessly before them, vast and untamed, but for the first time, Marcella felt a flicker of hope stir within her. Whatever awaited them on the mainland, she was ready to face it.

And she wasn't afraid to admit that she was scared. Because, as her father had said, it was normal. It meant she cared.

As the ship's crew bustled behind them, preparing for the night ahead, Marcella leaned her head on her father's shoulder. The sheer feel of her dad's presence was enough to make her feel safe and at ease, her irrational thoughts momentarily quieted by the steady rhythm of the waves.

Chapter Five

Around 20 miles north of Blackhevan, on the Island of Hammerdeep, the dwarves gathered in the great hall. A bastion carved from the very bones of the mountain, King Tholgar Ironfist sat at the head of a massive stone table. The table itself seemed to pulse with the essence of the mountain, its cold surface etched with the history of his people. The dim glow of lanterns flickered above, casting dancing shadows that mirrored the unease among the assembled council. Tholgar's thick fingers drummed a steady rhythm against the stone, his piercing gaze fixed upon the weathered map of Skell sprawled before him, now illuminated as if by some newfound clarity. Around the table, his trusted advisors sat in an anxious silence, their eyes flicking nervously towards the distant mainland. The air crackled with anticipation.

King Tholgar Ironfist is a robust dwarf, standing just over four feet tall but radiating an undeniable presence. His broad shoulders and muscular build reflect years of hard work. His thick, dark beard, interspersed with streaks of silver metal beads, and his deep-set blue eyes sparkle with wisdom and determination.

In the days of The High King Draegon, the dwarves had no formal king—only extraordinary leaders who rose to occasions. One of these remarkable individuals was Khorgar Ironfist, Tholgar's father. Khorgar was a towering figure known for his intelligence and fighting skills, both armed and unarmed. He wore intricately crafted dwarven armour fully glazed over with a centimetre of Obsidean, considered unbreakable by the master welders who forged it. A deep crimson cloak billowed behind him, its bold hue contrasting with the dark metal of his armour. At his side hung a mighty war hammer with sharps silver tips.

When the dwarves and humans were exiled from Skell by the elves, it marked the beginning of a desperate voyage for survival. Forced to leave their homeland, both races set sail in search of new shores, and Khorgar Ironfist took command of their journey. He captained the largest of the three ships they managed to steal from the elves—a vessel sturdy enough to weather the seas, though it bore the scars of previous battles.

Their initial goal was Blackhevan, a coastal city where they hoped to find refuge. However, upon reaching the city's shores, they discovered that the humans had already claimed it. The humans, led by their own exiled leaders, had arrived first, quickly securing what little land was available and fortifying their position. There was no room left for the dwarves, and tensions ran high. Rather than contest their claim, Khorgar chose another path. He knew that his people needed more than just a place to settle; they needed a stronghold to rebuild their future, away from any other race or clan. The dwarves could only trust each other.

Khorgar turned his gaze northward. He led the dwarves deeper to sea, steering their fleet through treacherous waters. The dwarven ships battled fierce winds and storms that lashed their sails and churned the sea into chaos. Khorgar's skills shone through; he handled the storms like a true captain. Standing at the helm, his hand gripped tightly around the ship's wheel, his leadership kept the crew focused and driven, his voice cutting through the storm as he reassured them of their destination.

Khorgar saw potential in Hammerdeep, a rugged island 20 miles north of Blackhevan, where others saw only challenges. Khorgar led the fleet safely to shore, and when the dwarves finally set foot on Hammerdeep, he wasted no time; his natural leadership took charge. Khorgar immediately began organising his people, leading the first hunts into the dense forests along the island's coastlines. Under his guidance, skilled trackers and warriors found game and fruit to feed the community, ensuring no dwarf went hungry despite the unfamiliar terrain.

Khorgar was more than just a hunter; he took command of the island's survival efforts. He oversaw the construction of their first homes, directing teams to carve shelters into the mountainside of Grimstone, Hammerdeep's largest peak. These homes, hewn from the mountain's rock, became popular with the new inhabitants of Hammerdeep; everyone wanted to move into the mountain. Khorgar envisioned Hammerdeep not just as a refuge but as a fortress—a place where dwarves could rebuild their pride and dignity.

He organised mining operations, directing craftsmen deep into the mountain to uncover rich veins of iron and precious metals that would fuel their industry. Under his leadership, Hammerdeep transformed from a temporary sanctuary into a thriving dwarven stronghold. His tireless work ethic inspired his people, and soon, they voted him King, not just out of necessity but out of loyalty and respect. He had earnt the right; in the hearts of his people, Khorgar had saved them.

He established training grounds for warriors to ensure every able-bodied dwarf could defend their new home whilst also promoting the traditional arts of smithing and stonecraft that defined their culture. Khorgar's foresight and authority laid the foundation for what would become one of the greatest dwarven strongholds in history.

Much like his father, Tholgar commanded respect with his authoritative demeanour, embodying the spirit of a warrior king. His leadership is spearheaded by honour and justice, always prioritising the well-being of his Kingdom and its people, making him a beloved figure among his subjects.

"This isn't some trick of the eye, is it?" Kozna Duhnmar, Tholgar's eldest advisor, spoke first, his voice laced with disbelief. His beard, streaked with silver, quivered slightly as he leaned forward, his brow furrowed. "I've heard strange tales of Skell in my day, but this... It's as if the very fabric of our world has turned upside down."

Tholgar's deep voice rumbled like distant thunder, steady and unwavering. "Nay, it's no trick. Elaena's magic has faded. The sky flickered for days, and now, our land returns to us. We cannot squander time pondering the whys. Action is what we need; my guess is the witch is either dead or has lost the plot." Tholgar Ironfist leaned closer to the map, and he studied it intensely.

"Aye, but how? The sea between us is perilous, and if the magic was tied to Elaena's life, who knows what else might be awakening on Skell?" replied Konza.

Tholgar's gaze narrowed, his features hardening like granite. "We go back. Simple as that. The elves may still linger, but without their queen, their hold has weakened. They won't rule uncontested for long. We'll send scouts first—a small party to gauge the situation—then we'll move in force."

"What of the others?" a younger Dwarf asked hesitantly from the far end of the table, his voice barely above a whisper. "The Orks, the Humans, the Snowpeople? They've seen Skell return as well. If we venture alone, we will be blind."

Tholgar slammed his fist against the table, the sound echoing through the hall like the roar of a mountain's awakening. "Let them come. The Dwarves of Hammerdeep do not cower behind walls. But first, we must understand what awaits us. Baldric Endholl, ready a ship—small, swift. We need eyes on the mainland before we make our move."

Badric nodded, determination replacing his earlier internal anxiety. "Yes, your Majesty. We'll uncover what waits for us by sunrise."

Chapter Six

On the rugged shores of Gruk'Thor Island, the orks of the Redaxe Clan gathered beneath the ominous black banner that billowed in the salty breeze. The air was thick with the acrid scent of smoke as the fires of their council blazed fiercely, illuminating their grim faces with flickering orange light. Shadows danced across the rocky ground, twisting and turning like the restless spirits of their ancestors.

The rise of the Redaxe Clan as the dominant force on Gruk'Thor Island was born from the brutal chaos of early ork history on the island. When the orks first arrived after exile from Skell, the clans were wild and divided. Rivalries formed deep, and betrayal was common. There was no unity, no order—only chaos as the clans clashed for supremacy in a land that had no rulers.

For years, the island was stained with ork blood. Clans that had once fought side by side turned on each other, their hunger for power outweighing any sense of kinship. Battles broke out over territory, resources, and pride, with shifting alliances that could turn in an instant. Trust was rare, and treachery lurked behind every handshake. It was a time of brutality, where only the strongest or most cunning survived.

At the heart of this savage power struggle, the Redaxe Clan emerged. Known for their intelligence in battle and unyielding leadership, the Redaxes, under their fierce chieftain, Ugbolo Ironfang, began to shape the island's fate. Ugbolo had a mind for strategy, and unlike many of his rivals, he saw that endless fighting would destroy them all. He knew that the only way to conquer the island was to unite the orks, not through words, but through fear and tactical prowess.

The Redaxe Clan became infamous for their relentless raids. Eventually, after countless battles, betrayals, and bloodshed, they stood unchallenged. The once-fractured ork clans were forced to fall in line under their banner. Those clans who swore fealty were spared, but at a price: they became lesser clans, forever under the rule of the Redaxes. Their newfound unity was not born from peace or diplomacy but from raw power, and that power solidified the Redaxes' place at the top.

Even Gron Ironfang, Urag's successor, understood the precarious nature of their dominance. The island, now under Redaxe's control, was more stable, but the memory of chaos was fresh. Gron, a chieftain both brutal and wise, knew that their strength could only hold if the clans remained united in purpose. The Redaxe Clan ruled with an iron fist, but they also took calculated steps to maintain order and ensure that no other clan could rise to challenge them.

After years of Ironfang rule, the other houses on the island started to accept their place, the people of Gruk'Thor started to love and respect the chieftain as the orks were living good lives, and the people appreciated that the control brought a good quality of life.

At the centre of this fierce gathering stood Gron Ironfang, the formidable chieftain of the Orks. His towering figure, broad and muscular, seemed to dominate the very space around him, casting a long shadow that enveloped his gathered kin. Gron's tusks jutted from his lower jaw, catching the firelight as he surveyed his comrades with a fierce intensity." The sky flickers, and now the land we were banished from returns," he growled, his voice a low rumble, thick with suspicion and defiance. "This is no coincidence. Skell is ours by right. We were exiled, but the elves no longer wield the magic that once kept us at bay."

Among the throng, a grizzled ork named Raggok stepped forward, his face scarred from countless fighting in training. He spat into the fire, the embers hissing as they met his saliva. "If the magic's gone, the elves are weaker than ever. Now's the time to strike. We take back what was stolen from us!" His voice rang with a fervour that stirred the spirits of the gathered warriors. Gron raised a massive hand, silencing the eager murmurs. "Not yet. The mainland may have reappeared, but we do not know what lies there. The Dwarves, the Humans, the Snowpeople—they will also be moving to reclaim what is theirs. We must be cunning."

"Raggok growled in frustration but bowed his head in submission, his muscles tensing with restrained impatience. "What's the plan, then?"

Gron's gaze shifted, his eyes narrowing as he scanned the flickering flames. Each flicker reflected the sharpness of his mind, calculating and strategic. "We send scouts first. A small raiding party to the northern shores. They will sail under the cloak of night, slipping in and out without a trace. I want to know if the elves are lying in wait for us or if they have already crumbled under the weight of their arrogance. Then, we attack."

A thunderous roar of approval erupted from the gathered Orks, their voices blending into a savage chorus that echoed across the rocky landscape. Yet Gron raised his hand once more, commanding their attention. "If the other factions are on the move, we will watch them too. They have waited as long as we have to return. Let them think they have the upper hand; when the moment is right, we shall strike when they are weakest."

The fire crackled, and the air thickened with anticipation as the warriors absorbed Gron's words; their spirits.

Chapter Seven

The half-human, half-wolf High Priestess Ylvana stood at the icy balcony of Jotungard's towering citadel, her breath crystallising in the frigid air as she glared at the distant outline of Skell. Around her, the snowpeople gathered, a wall of pale faces and fierce eyes, their hulking, seven-foot frames looming in the dim, cold light of the northern stars.

Her loyal army and subjects glared up at their ferocious leader, ready to be inspired. A young cub stared up at the Priestess with his jaw touching the floor, eyes as wide as an elven sword, in disbelief that he was so close to her. He could see her stolen golden elven armour, which gave a fierce and enigmatic presence and gleamed brilliantly, yet it seemed almost out of place on her wild and untamed figure. Nevertheless, she looked like a tough fight. Her face, though humanoid, carries the sharp angles of a wolf, with a short, wolfish snout and pointed ears poking through her thick mane of hair. Her skin, covered in a layer of silvery fur, glistens faintly, reflecting the cold intensity of her icy blue eyes. The child looked directly into her eyes; into her eyes, he could see shards of the frozen sky; it was like they held the depths of winter within them—cold, calculating, yet hypnotic. The young boy carried on assessing the High Priestess Ylvana, taking it all in before someone stepped in front of him, blocking the view. Around her waist, she carried a belt of shimmering elven gold adorned with bones, feathers, and small trophies of her own—each one a sign of her victories. Despite the heavy armour, she moves with the fluidity of a predator, silent and swift. Her powerful legs, covered in thick fur, are visible beneath the plates of armour that end just above her knees, allowing her the freedom to leap and run with the speed of a wolf. Her clawed feet barely make a sound, even in the heaviest of armour, and a long, lupine tail sways behind her, its silver-grey fur contrasting with the golden sheen of the armour.

She is a being of both beauty and terror—a creature of the wild, draped in the spoils of a more civilised race, her icy gaze revealing a deep, cold cunning. Her presence commands both awe and fear, and her armour, once a symbol of elven nobility, now serves as a testament to her untamed power and triumph over the delicate forces of order.

The snow people of Jotungard were a unique and complex society, divided sharply into two tiers based on the physical traits they were born with. As a race of half-wolf, half-human beings, their appearance determined not only their place in the community but also their role in the survival of their harsh, frozen world. The hierarchy was clear: those who were born with more wolf-like features, known as full borns, had fur-covered bodies, elongated snouts, sharp claws, and powerful, lupine legs—were revered as the elite warriors and soldiers of the snow people. These wolf-dominant individuals, like their ferocious High Priestess Ylvana, embodied the raw power and predatory grace that the snow people valued most. They were seen as the true protectors of their race, naturally suited for battle and patrolling the treacherous, icy wilderness that surrounded Jotungard.

On the other hand, those born with more human features, known as half-borns, had skin instead of fur, shorter, less animalistic faces, and fewer visible wolf traits—were regarded as second-class citizens. Whilst they still possessed the agility, strength, and heightened senses of their wolf heritage, their appearance condemned them to a life of servitude and labour within the community. These more human-looking snow people were expected to take on the essential yet less glorified roles of hunters, gatherers, and protectors of their families. They were the ones who braved the frozen forests to bring back food, hunted the wild animals that roamed the tundras, and ensured their households were warm and fed, but they were never allowed to rise to the prestigious rank of soldier.

This division ran deep within their society. Despite their abilities, those who looked more human were never truly seen as equals to their wolf-like counterparts. They were not allowed to join the ranks of the elite soldiers, nor could they hold positions of power. Instead, they were relegated to supporting roles—important for the community's survival but uncelebrated and often overlooked. These individuals, though capable of great feats, were seen as unworthy of the same respect as their wolf-dominant kin.

Even the young among the snow people understood this division. From birth, it was clear who would become a soldier and who would be destined to serve in the shadows, protecting the village from less visible threats whilst remaining largely invisible themselves. This rigid social structure was accepted as natural law among the snow people, who valued strength, ferocity, and wolf-like characteristics above all else.

"The magic that hid Skell is gone!" Ylvana spat, her voice cutting through the biting wind like a jagged shard of ice. "The land of our ancestors lies bare before us, and the time for us to reclaim it is now!"

Beside her, Toric, a powerful warrior with muscles forged in the harshest winters, tightened his grip on his frost-forged spear, his expression a mask of barely contained fury. "The elves are vulnerable without Elaena's magic. But do we know what has become of those treacherous vermin?" His voice dripped with hatred, each word laced with the promise of violence.

Ylvana's icy blue eyes flickered with ancient knowledge, but her lips curled into a snarl. "We will not be the first to set foot on Skell. We are not the only predators lurking in the shadows. The Humans, the Dwarves, the Orks—they all scent blood and vengeance like a pack on the hunt. They'll move before we do, and they'll move with fury."

Toric's growl rumbled like thunder in the frozen air. "And what of us, then? Are we to sit idly by whilst others stake their claim? Do we wait for the storm to pass, or do we unleash the power of our army?" His knuckles whitened around the spear, the wood creaking under the pressure of his fury.

Ylvana turned to him, her gaze as cold as the frozen sea that surrounded their island, and a feral light sparked in her eyes. "We send an army—silent, swift, merciless. The snowpeople have always moved unseen, like the chill that creeps into your bones. We will watch from the shadows, revelling in the chaos that unfolds. Only when the time is right will we descend upon them, and when we do, it will be with the full force of our rage. They will not see us coming until it's too late; an early strike will see us victorious."

A low growl rippled through the gathered snowpeople, a primal promise of what was to come. The air crackled with anticipation, the promise of blood and conquest hanging thick in the icy atmosphere.

Chapter Eight

As the exiled factions readied their ships, the sea buzzed with fervent activity, a symphony of preparation echoing across the waters. By dawn, fleets of scouting parties had launched from each island, their sails billowing like the spirits of those they carried.

From Hammerdeep, the determined Dwarves dispatched their swiftest longboat, a sleek vessel designed for speed. At the helm was Tholgar Ironfist, a seasoned leader known for his unyielding courage and keen sense of navigation. With a crew of hardened warriors, they charted a course towards Selthor shore, their eyes set on the horizon as the first light of day broke over the waves.

To the south, on the beaches of Blackhevan. The humans, led by King Cael, were preparing to embark. The King had decided to take some extra last-minute precautions to make sure he and his daughter returned alive. Despite her lack of sailing knowledge, she was resolved to see her way and go with them. The boats were filled to the brim with the King's most trusted knights, each one sworn to protect the princess and ensure her safe return.

The air was thick with tension as they loaded supplies and armour, the knights exchanging nervous glances whilst reassuring their leader.

Meanwhile, the Orks were plotting under the cloak of darkness. A small scouting vessel slipped silently from the shores south of Skell, its crew moving with the stealth of shadows. Their mission was clear: infiltrate the enemy's territory and return without detection. The Orks, known for their cunning and ferocity, embraced the cover of night as their ally.

Farther north, the Snow People of Jotungard had already set sail, their ships gliding effortlessly on the icy winds. Clad in ancient, stolen elven armour that shimmered with a ghostly hue, they moved like spectres through the mist-shrouded northern sea. Unlike the other factions, they did not send a scouting party; the entire population of Jotungard had embarked on this voyage. Nearly 10,000 snowpeople made the short journey across the Arctic waters. With a history steeped in the lands they were returning to, The north of Skell was their ancestral homeland, inhabited for nearly a thousand years. They were uniquely adapted to the harsh conditions of their journey alongside the frost giants, who would most likely not bother them upon arrival. For them, settling upon familiar shores would pose no challenge; they were ready to reclaim what was rightfully theirs.

All eyes were on Skell, now no longer a tale of the past but a land waiting to be reclaimed. The factions were coming, and the war that had been brewing for 120 years was about to ignite. The seas around Skell churned as the scouting parties of the exiled factions advanced, each group sailing under the ominous skies that had once been veiled by the magic of Queen Elaena. As they approached the long-hidden mainland, the sense of excitement had grown into unease, which was growing with each passing moment.

The first to encounter trouble were the Dwarves. King Tholgar Ironfists longboat cut through the waters at a rapid pace, his crew of seasoned scouts hardened by years of survival in the rugged lands of Hammerdeep. As they neared the southern coastline of Skell, the jagged mountains and tropical forests came into view. Strange, exotic birds circled high above the trees, their calls echoing across the waves.

“Skell looks...different to what I’d have imaged,” King Tholgar Ironfist muttered, gazing up at the unfamiliar terrain. The mountains, once home to their ancestors’ mines, now seemed overgrown with vines and vegetation. “What the fuck happened here?”

Before anyone could respond, a loud screech pierced the air. Baldric’s head snapped upward just in time to see the shadow of something massive sweeping down from the clouds.

“By the ancestors...!” one of the Dwarves yelled, pointing skyward.

Suddenly, a monstrous figure broke through the cloud cover, its wingspan larger than any bird known to man. Pterodactyls.

"Get down!" Tholgar roared, his voice a desperate shout over the chaos. The crew, a motley assembly of scouts, scrambled to respond. Panic spread like wildfire, the air thick with fear as the first pterodactyl swooped low, its talons outstretched, glinting like knives in the sunlight. King Tholgar had read about these creatures in old texts—beasts that ruled the skies aeons before humanity even dared to dream of flight. He had dismissed those tales as mere fantasy, stories woven into the fabric of myth to entertain children by the hearth. But now, standing at the helm of his ship, he realised how terribly mistaken he had been.

A Dwarf screamed, his voice piercing through the cacophony as the monstrous beak clamped around him, lifting him effortlessly from the deck. The sheer power of the creature was awe-inspiring and terrifying. It was a visceral reminder of nature's indifference to the lives of mortals. The Dwarf flailed helplessly, his eyes wide with terror, as the pterodactyl ascended into the blue abyss, its wings beating furiously. The ship lurched beneath them, the crew members grasping at ropes and masts, desperate to keep their footing. With a sickening crack of a harpoon, the creature was blown to bits, and the released captive was left plummeting into the dark sea below, a splash that sent waves cascading over the ship's side. Baldric's heart sank with him, but there was no time for grief. He had to act.

"Grab more harpoons!" he shouted, his voice rising above the chaos. "We can't let them pick us off one by one!" He felt the weight of responsibility settles on his shoulders. The crew was counting on him, and he refused to let fear govern his actions. Amidst the shouts and scrambling, a pair of elder Dwarves moved with grace, their hands deftly retrieving the harpoons from the storage hold. They nodded at their leader with determination in their eyes.

He could see their resolve mirrored in the faces of the Dwarves, even as panic coursed through their veins. Each crew member was driven by a selfish primal instinct to survive whilst remembering their selfless loyalty to one another.

King Tholgar prepared himself; another pterodactyl swooped down, its enormous wings casting a shadow over the boat once more. This time, the crew was ready. With a swift motion, he launched a harpoon towards the beast. It struck true, piercing the leathery flesh, and the creature let out a deafening screech that echoed across the water.

Tholgar felt a rush of adrenaline, but the victory was short-lived. The creature veered violently, dragging the ship slightly off course. The harpoon line began to slacken, but the beast's death throes only seemed to agitate the others in the sky. A formation of pterodactyls circled, their eyes fixed on the ship as if they could sense the blood in the water—their natural instinct to hunt ignited.

“Reload!” he shouted, urgency rising in his voice. He could feel the weight of each passing second; they were running out of time. Another Dwarf, bold yet reckless, threw himself onto the deck, readying another harpoon. With a primal yell, he launched it into the sky. The harpoon sailed through the air but missed its mark, the pterodactyl deftly dodging. Tholgar cursed under his breath. They needed a plan—a way to outsmart the very beasts that had once ruled the skies.

The air froze with tension, every crew member on edge, hearts pounding in synchrony. They were not just fighting for their lives but also for the bond they shared, forged through countless storms and sea monsters in their previous adventures. At that moment, King Tholgar made a silent promise to honour every soul aboard his ship.

“Form a line! Keep your eyes up!” he commanded, galvanising the crew. They were not simply prey; they were a united front against an ancient terror. As the pterodactyls dove again, they would fight back with all their might, for the sky was vast, but their courage was boundless.

The other factions weren’t spared either. Across the waters, The Orks aboard King Gron Ironfang’s raiding vessel braced themselves as the skies darkened with the shadow of circling pterodactyls. The ship, though swift, seemed minuscule against the formidable forces descending from above. Gron stood at the helm, his muscular frame silhouetted against the fading sun, determination etched across his scarred face.

"Brace yourselves!" he shouted, his voice booming over the cacophony of flapping wings and frantic cries. The Orks, a chaotic blend of green skin and rugged armour, responded with grunts and shouts, quickly moving to their battle stations. They were seasoned warriors accustomed to skirmishes, but these ancient creatures were unlike anything they had faced before. As the first pterodactyl swooped down, its wings casting a dark shadow over the deck, Gron felt a surge of adrenaline. The beast's sharp beak glistened ominously, its talons extended like daggers. With a deafening screech, it lunged at the nearest Ork, narrowly missing him as he ducked and rolled to safety.

"Get your axes!" Gron roared, brandishing his own massive weapon, the blade gleaming in the waning light. "Fight like true warriors of Gruk'Thor!" The Orks rallied, and their primal instincts ignited. Several charged forward, jagged blades raised high, whilst others prepared the ship's deck-mounted cannons. One brave Ork, Wout, a burly figure with a makeshift helm adorned with feathers, hurled a spear at the incoming creature. The spear struck true, embedding itself into the pterodactyl's wing. With a furious screech, the beast spiralled into a nearby mast, the impact sending splinters flying and leaving it dazed.

"Finish it!" Gron shouted, eyes blazing with the thrill of battle. The Orks surged forward, surrounding the wounded creature. Wout was the first to reach it, swinging his axe with ferocity, cleaving through flesh and feathers. The pterodactyl thrashed wildly, but the combined strength of the Orks was too much. With a final, anguished cry, it collapsed onto the deck, blood pooling around its massive body.

"More incoming!" one of the lookout Orks shouted, pointing skyward. Gron turned just in time to see a formation of pterodactyls swooping down in unison, their eyes locked onto the ship as if sensing the scent of blood.

"Deck-mounted cannons! get them fucking loaded up!" Gron commanded, his voice steady despite the chaos. The crew scrambled, their hands moving deftly to prepare the cannons for a volley. Just as the first of the pterodactyls dove down, Gron positioned himself at the helm of the nearest cannon.

"Fire!" he roared, and the cannon boomed, sending a cannonball hurtling into the air. It struck one of the pterodactyls mid-dive, exploding in a shower of feathers and blood. The remaining beasts screeched in outrage, their fury palpable as they regrouped for another assault.

"Steady!" Gron urged as he glanced around at his crew, their faces fierce with determination. The Orks, though rough and rowdy, shared a bond forged in battle. They knew their lives depended on each other now.

As the next wave of pterodactyls dove in, Gron barked orders: “Form a line! Protect the cannons!”

The crew spread out, creating a barrier between the beasts and their artillery. The first pterodactyl struck, its talons raking across the deck as it tried to land. Gron swung his axe, catching the beast in its side. The beast howled in pain, staggering backwards.

The deck became a whirlwind of motion as Orks fought with reckless abandon. They worked in unison, dodging and striking, each blow fueled by adrenaline. One ork managed to grab a harpoon and thrust it towards another pterodactyl, striking it squarely in the chest. It let out a shriek before plummeting into the sea, its wings flailing in a desperate attempt to stay airborne.

With each downed creature, the morale of the Orks soared. Gron rallied them, his voice a battle cry. “For the Ironfang! We are stronger than these beasts!” The Orks roared in response, their spirits ignited by his words. The tide of battle shifted as they began to gain the upper hand. With renewed vigour, they targeted the remaining pterodactyls, their movements more coordinated. Wout, now wielding a pair of jagged blades, danced through the fray, striking at any beast that dared come close.

“Look out!” another ork shouted as a pterodactyl swooped low, aiming straight for Gron. In a moment of instinct, he ducked just in time, feeling the rush of wind as the creature passed overhead. It screeched angrily, circling for another dive. “Not this time!” Gron shouted, raising his axe high. He waited until the last possible moment before swinging downward as the beast descended again, catching it mid-dive. The creature let out a final cry before crashing onto the deck, defeated.

As the last of the pterodactyls fell, silence enveloped the ship, broken only by the heavy breathing of the Orks. Gron looked around at his crew, their faces smeared with blood and victory. They had fought not just for survival but to protect their honour, proving themselves against an ancient menace.

“Tend the injured!” Gron commanded, a look of anger across his face. “We have to keep everyone fit; we need numbers!” The Orks tended to the injured as commanded, and they also began to strip the fallen beasts of their feathers and claws, trophies of their hard-fought victory.

On the Humans’ boat, Marcella raised her shield as another pterodactyl dive-bombed, its sharp beak grazing her arm before her sword found its neck. The creature screeched in agony, its wings flapping wildly as it struggled against the fatal blow. “These creatures are supposed to be myths!” she shouted, disbelief etched on her face as she wiped the blood from her cheek.

“They’ve never been myths,” King Cael replied, his voice steady despite the chaos around them.

He pulled an arrow from his quiver, nocked it with practised ease, and loosed it at another pterodactyl that swooped towards them. The arrow flew straight and true, striking the creature squarely in the chest. It let out a death cry, spiralling into the ocean below, its body crashing into the waves with a violent splash.

Marcella's heart raced, and her eyes watered as she scanned the tumultuous skies above. The ship rocked beneath her feet, and the salty sea spray mingled with the metallic scent of blood. "We need to regroup!" she shouted, her whimpering voice cutting through the din of chaos. "kill them!" She shouted.

The crew, a mix of seasoned warriors and new recruits, scrambled to obey. They tightened their formation, shields raised and weapons poised, each member bolstered by the sight of their comrades standing firm against the aerial onslaught. More pterodactyls circled overhead, their silhouettes darkening the sun as they prepared for another dive. Marcella felt a surge of fear but quickly quelled it. These beasts were no longer just tales told by old sailors; they were here, hunting them, and it was their job to fight back. "Stay sharp!" she called, her voice now steady. "They'll come for us again!"

As if on cue, two pterodactyls launched themselves from the clouds, talons extended, and beaks bared. Marcella steeled herself, heart pounding, and locked eyes with her father. He nodded, and they both prepared for the oncoming assault.

One of the pterodactyls dove straight for Marcella, its wings slicing through the air with a whooshing sound. She swung her shield upward just in time, deflecting the beast's beak as it lunged. The impact rattled her bones, but she held firm, feeling the force of its weight against her. With a swift motion, she countered, slashing her sword upward and catching the creature's neck. Blood sprayed, and it spiralled away, crashing into the sea with a thunderous splash.

"Good shot!" King Cael yelled, already loading another arrow. His focus never wavered, eyes darting as he tracked the movements of the remaining creatures. "But there are more! Watch your backs!"

Princess Marcella turned just in time to see another pterodactyl swooping low, aiming for one of the younger recruits who stood frozen in fear. Without thinking, she charged forward. "Get down!" she yelled, throwing herself in front of him. She raised her shield again, bracing for the impact.

The creature collided with her shield, the force almost knocking her off her feet. "Princess!" the recruit cried, his voice trembling.

"Focus!" she shouted back, her eyes fierce. She shifted her weight and swung her sword, cutting deep into the creature's side. It screeched in pain, flapping its wings in a desperate attempt to escape. With one final blow, Princess Marcella severed its head, and it dropped lifelessly onto the deck.

Panting, she turned to the recruit. "You have to fight! Don't let fear control you! I'm okay. Don't worry about me."

He nodded, fear still glimmering in his eyes but a flicker of determination igniting within him. "It's my duty to worry about you, Princess!"

The battle raged on, the air thick with the cries of the beasts and the shouts of the Humans. Cael continued to fire arrows with remarkable accuracy, each shot striking down a pterodactyl before it could reach the deck. Marcella fought beside him, pushing back against the relentless tide of creatures.

One of the archers shouted from the back, "We're losing men quickly! They're coming in too fast!"

"Then we need to create space!" Cael replied, gesturing to the nearest deck-mounted cannon so that they could pivot to the sky. "Load it up! We need firepower!"

The crew quickly responded, moving to the cannon and preparing it for a shot. Princes Marcella and King Cael worked to keep the remaining pterodactyls at bay, dodging and slashing, the rhythm of battle becoming second nature.

When the deck-mounted cannon was primed, King Cael shouted, "Fire!"

The artillery roared to life, the blast echoing across the water. A massive projectile struck one of the pterodactyls mid-dive, exploding in a shower of feathers and blood. The beast crumpled, spiralling into the depths of the ocean, and a wave of relief washed over the crew.

“Keep firing!” Marcella called, her voice rising above the chaos. “We can’t let up!” They worked in unison, the cannon firing again and again, each blast clearing a path through the swarm of creatures. But Marcella could see that their numbers were still overwhelming. Pterodactyls circled overhead, watching for any sign of weakness, and she knew they needed to take decisive action. “Father, we need to move to the edge of the deck!” Marcella shouted. “If we can funnel them into a tighter space, we can deal with them more easily!”

“Right!” he agreed, his eyes blazing with determination. “Everyone! To the starboard side!” The crew shifted, moving as a unit towards the edge of the deck. Marcella felt the adrenaline surging through her, and as they reached the starboard side, she raised her sword high. “Form up! Let them come to us!” With a final, deafening roar, the pterodactyls dove down, drawn to the Humans’ shifting formation. They soared closer, talons outstretched, and Marcella felt the rush of wind as one swooped down towards her. She sidestepped, slashing her sword horizontally as the beast flew past.

In that instant, she caught sight of her father at her side, losing arrow after arrow, his aim unwavering. Together, they fought back against the tide of beasts;

their movements synchronised as they fended off each incoming attack. "Marcella!" King Cael shouted, pointing to a particularly large pterodactyl that was circling above. "That one's leading the pack! If we take it down, the others may scatter!" "Then we need to bring it down!" she yelled back, determination surging within her. As the creature dove, the King readied an arrow, taking careful aim. "On my mark!" Marcella nodded, positioning herself to distract the beast as it swooped in. When it was close, she raised her shield, preparing for the impact. The pterodactyl slammed into her shield, but she held firm, adrenaline fueling her strength.

"Now!" King Cael shouted, letting loose his arrow.

The arrow flew true, striking the pterodactyl in the wing. It screeched, tumbling off course and crashing onto the deck. Seizing the opportunity, Marcella charged forward, delivering a decisive blow with her sword. The creature fell still, and with its death, an eerie silence settled over the ship.

"Is it over?" one of the soldiers asked, breathless.

"For now," Cael replied, scanning the horizon. "But we must be ready for anything."

Marcella looked around at her comrades, their faces smeared with sweat and blood but their spirits unbroken. "We did it," she breathed, a wave of relief washing over her.

"We did," Cael agreed, clapping her shoulder. "But we can't let our guard down. The legends may be true, but so is our strength. Together, we'll face whatever comes next."

As the ship drifted into calmer waters, Marcella felt a new resolve forming within her. They had faced the impossible, and they had fought not just for survival but for each other.

Chapter Nine

Whilst the pterodactyls ravaged the skies, the Orks faced an even more terrifying foe from the depths.

As Gron Ironfang stood tall at the bow of his ship, watching the last of the flying creatures fall, the water around the ship began to ripple unnaturally. The sea suddenly grew calm, eerily so, as though holding its breath.

"Something's wrong," Raggok muttered.

The ocean beneath them erupted in a violent surge. From the depths of the sea came a creature of legend, a serpentine beast with scales darker than night and eyes that glowed like burning coals. Thraxis, the famous and feared ancient sea serpent. Its head rose high above the ship, easily fifty feet into the air, its jaws wide enough to swallow a man whole.

"It's real..." Gron whispered as his eyes expanded along with his jaw. Thraxis lunged.

The Orks scattered across the deck, narrowly avoiding the massive jaws as they crashed into the side of the ship. Wood splintered, and the vessel rocked violently. Several Orks were thrown into the sea, their screams quickly silenced by the serpent's thrashing coils. Gron regained his footing and roared, "Man, the harpoons! Aim for its head!"

The Orks rushed to the ship's machinery—massive steel harpoon launchers mounted on either side of the vessel. The serpent struck again, but this time, they were ready. With a deafening thud, a harpoon fired, embedding itself deep into Thraxis' neck. The beast shrieked, piercing the sky and thrashing wildly, but the Orks held firm.

Gron Ironfang turned to the Chaplin of fire, who controlled the dragites, small bat-sized creatures with pointy horns who could breathe fire. "Chaplin, where are your dragites? Get them out here and help," he screamed in his deep and raspy voice. His attention then quickly shifted back to the orks. "Pull it down!" Gron ordered, and with great effort, the crew began reeling the serpent in. Thraxis writhed, its enormous tail crashing into the sea, creating waves that threatened to capsize the ship. But Gron, eyes wild and fury, leapt onto the creature's head and started repeatedly driving his battle axe deep between its eyes.

With a final, ear-splitting wail, the serpent's body went limp, sinking slowly beneath the waves. The Orks, battered but victorious, roared in triumph.

But their victory was short-lived. As the last echoes of the serpent's wail faded into the depths, an unsettling silence enveloped the crew. Gron, still panting from the adrenaline, turned to survey his comrades. The deck was strewn with the bodies of their fallen, the remnants of their brave fight against both the pterodactyls and Thraxis.

"Look around!" Gron bellowed, his voice thick with anger and despair. "We've lost too many. We can't stay here; it's only a matter of time before another beast comes for us!"

Raggok, his second-in-command, nodded grimly, his face smeared with the grime of battle. "We need reinforcements. We can't take on any more of these monsters alone. We should retreat, gather more of our kin, and come back with numbers."

The remaining Orks, weary but resolute, began to murmur in agreement. Many of them had already lost family and friends in the harrowing fight, and the thought of returning home to rally their kind filled them with a flicker of hope.

Gron paced the deck, the salty breeze whipping through his hair. "Aye, home it is then! We'll gather the rest of the clan and return with a vengeance. We'll revenge the fallen and make them proud!"

With a newfound determination, the Orks set to work. They pulled the ship's sails, catching the wind that would carry them back to their homeland. A long journey was ahead for them, but at least they had time to rest their bruised and beaten bodies.

As the coastline came into view, Gron felt a pang of relief. Their home was a fortress—a place where they could gather strength, forge weapons, and prepare for the inevitable battles ahead. As they grew closer, the figure of Ork-like shadows started to appear. Natives waited like loyal dogs who were surely eager to hear of their success. Just what Gron didn't want or need. He was downbeat and embarrassed; he was dreading speaking of their failure.

After the day-long journey home, they finally docked; Gron was met by a gathering of concerned faces. He stepped off the ship, his massive frame towering over the gathered crowd of Orks; he felt the weight of their expectant stares. His chest, broad and battle-scarred, rose as he drew in a deep breath, standing tall despite the weariness of battle clinging to his bones. His fierce, yellow eyes swept over the sea of faces—his people. Brothers, sisters, and kin who had fought alongside him or waited for news of triumph, but what he had to offer was something heavier than glory.

He stepped forward, his voice booming like the crash of thunder: "Listen to me!" Gron began, his voice raw with honesty and the rasp of battle. "You see the scars on our ship, the blood on our hands. This was no victory, no triumph to boast about. The pterodactyls in the skies were nothing compared to what came from below. Thraxis, the ancient serpent, rose from the depths to claim us, and though we fought like beasts, we lost good warriors. Too many."

A hush fell over the gathered Orks, their eyes wide with fear and respect for the name of Thraxis. The weight of the losses echoed in the silence, pressing down like a heavy stone.

Gron's gaze hardened, his posture straight and unyielding. "Look around you. We returned, but not all of us did. The sea claimed our kin, and their blood stained our memories. We were outmatched and outnumbered. I won't lie to you; we faced something we shouldn't have with the numbers we had. We bled, but we won."

His words cut through the air, cold and real. He wasn't here to inspire with false promises; he was here to remind them of their reality. But in that raw honesty, there was a flicker of something else.

"But hear this!" Gron's voice rose, the fire of determination lighting in his eyes. "We may have retreated today, but that doesn't mean we've been defeated. We will not be broken by fear! Thraxis was no common beast, and even **he** fell before our strength. **We** murdered the serpent, cut him down, and watched him sink beneath the waves. His body rests at the bottom of the sea because **we** stood our ground!"

The crowd murmured, a low rumble of respect stirring through them. Gron took a step closer to his people, his hands clenched into fists.

"But we need more than strength—we need numbers. We need to stand as one, not as scattered clans. We will gather our warriors, forge weapons stronger than any before, and return to that cursed sea; we will arrive on the shores of Skell. We'll avenge the fallen, not just with rage, but with the power of all united!"

The Orks began to growl in approval, a low, rising sound of growing resolve.

Gron looked around, his voice softer now but filled with conviction. "I swear to you—next time, we will be ready for whatever else is out there; once we go, we are not coming back until the elves are dead. Next time, we'll come for blood, and we'll hit the elves hard. We fight for those we lost, for those we love. And we fight because no monster, no beast, no force on this earth will keep the Orks from claiming what's ours."

The crowd erupted in a roar of agreement, fists raised high. Gron nodded once, his chest swelling with pride—not for himself, but for the strength of his people. Despite their losses, despite the battle that still loomed ahead, he knew that together, they would be unstoppable.

"Gron!" shouted Zarruk, a burly ork with a fiery temper. "What in the world did you face out there? Is it true? A sea serpent?"

"More than that," Gron replied, grimly recounting their harrowing encounters. He spoke of the pterodactyls and Thraxis, watching as the expressions of disbelief morphed into determination. "We need every ork we can muster. We've lost too many already."

With a rallying cry, the Orks sprang into action. Scouts were sent to nearby villages, calling upon every clan to gather. The forge was lit, fires crackling as weapons were reforged and Armour mended. Gron could feel the energy of his people rising—a collective spirit that would not be easily extinguished.

Days turned into nights as the Orks trained and prepared. Gron stood atop a makeshift platform, addressing the gathered warriors. "We will not cower in fear! We are Orks, and we fight for our kin and our land. We'll return to the sea and hunt down that beast! We will show the elves and any others that threaten us the fury of our might!"

Finally, after weeks, the day arrived when the fleet of ork ships—now bolstered by reinforcements—set sail once more. Gron stood at the helm, a fierce glint in his eyes. As the waves surged beneath them, he felt the weight of their losses and the strength of their resolve intertwine. They were not merely a band of warriors; they were a relentless tide, ready to reclaim their honour and confront the monsters of the deep.

"Let's show them what we're made of!" he shouted, and with that, they charged into the open sea, the horizon stretching before them, filled with both peril and promise.

Chapter Ten

Princess Marcella was the first to set foot on the sandy beach, her heart racing with wonder. “This isn’t the Skell I was told about,” she exclaimed, taking in the vivid colours and strange flora that surrounded her. Each flower seemed to pulse with life, each sound resonating like a whisper of adventure.

Behind her, King Cael followed, his brow furrowed in disbelief. “It’s as though time itself has changed this land,” he said, his voice low but edged with caution. “But we didn’t come here to marvel at the scenery. Stay sharp. There’s no telling what else the elves have left behind.” His words hung heavy in the air, a reminder that they were not merely explorers but intruders in a land that might harbour its own guardians.

As the scouting parties ventured inland, a sense of unease settled over them. The verdant landscape, whilst stunning, was littered with signs of something vast and powerful. Massive footprints—enormous and deeply imprinted into the soft earth—stretched before them, leading into the thick foliage. Marcellas’s gaze fell upon them, curiosity quickly turning to apprehension. “What could have made these?" she whispered to her fellow warriors, her voice barely breaking the stillness.

A few miles to the north, the Dwarven faction had just arrived on their own stretch of the coastline. Unlike the Humans, they were not captivated by the beauty of Skell but rather focused on unloading their supplies from the ship. The rugged Dwarves, seasoned from years of hard work, approached their task with efficiency, but their keen eyes were quickly drawn to the ominous signs around them.

Tholgar Ironfist sensed the weight of the air shift. His sharp gaze caught a movement in the distance—something massive and slow emerging from the shadows of the towering trees. "Hold," he cautioned his men, raising a hand. "Something's here..." The ground trembled underfoot, the very earth-shaking as colossal figures began to materialise from the underbrush.

Giants—massive beings that had once served the legendary Queen Elaena as her fierce guardians—stepped into view. Their skin appeared as weathered stone, each ridge and crevice telling tales of ages past. Their eyes glowed with a malevolence that sent a chill down Baldric's spine. They brandished enormous clubs that could level trees with a single swing.

The giants of Skell were a peaceful and wise race, towering beings who preferred solitude and the serenity of nature over the bustling affairs of smaller creatures. Unlike the tales that often painted giants as brutish or aggressive, these giants were largely calm, introspective, and deeply connected to the land they called home. Their refuge was hidden deep within the vast expanse of the Torreldane Woods, a thick and ancient forest untouched by human hands for centuries.

The giants made their homes around the oldest and largest tree in the entire forest, a towering behemoth whose branches seemed to touch the heavens. To most, this tree looked no different from the others—just another massive sentinel among the sea of trunks. However, to the giants, it was unmistakable, a sacred symbol and a centre point of their hidden camps. They gathered here in reverence, drawing strength from the tree's deep roots, which stretched for miles beneath the earth.

Though the giants were largely peaceful, they did not tolerate intrusions from smaller beings, whether human or animal. Any foragers, adventurers, or creatures that wandered too close to their camps would be met with intimidating tactics. The giants didn't harm trespassers but were adept at scaring them away. With their immense size and the natural camouflage of the forest, they could create thunderous noises, shake the trees, or even silently move in ways that would make a traveller believe the woods themselves had come alive to warn them off.

Years ago, their peaceful isolation was disrupted when they encountered Elaena. She showed the giants compassion and respect, and she quickly recognised their wisdom and potential as protectors of Skell. In return for their loyalty, she cast a series of enchantments to ensure their lives within the woods were easier and more comfortable.

Elaena made the trees surrounding their camps blossom with an abundance of food. Fruits, nuts, and berries grew year-round, giving the giants sustenance without the need to venture far from their hidden sanctuary. These enchanted trees produced far more than any natural plant could, ensuring the giants never had to leave their protected grounds to seek food. Additionally, Elaena used her magic to reshape the caves and grottos beneath the woods, making them vast and deep enough to comfortably shelter the giants. What once had been cramped and narrow spaces now stretched into enormous caverns, ideal for giants seeking refuge during storms or winter months.

In exchange for these magical blessings, Elaena asked the giants to serve as silent guardians of the land. Their task was simple but crucial: to patrol the edges of Torreldane Woods, keeping watch over the coastline and the borders of Skell. They were to remain hidden, unnoticed by those they observed, unless they saw danger approaching from foreign lands. Should an outsider attempt to enter Skell, the Giants were to act as its first line of defence. Whilst they were rarely called to fight, their mere presence was often enough to deter invaders or unwanted visitors.

Despite their relatively small number—no more than forty giants—their strength and size made them more than enough to protect the vast stretches of forest and coastline. Forty giants, hidden within the towering trees and deep caves, were an unstoppable force if ever called upon. Their wisdom and Elaena's enchantments ensured that they lived in harmony with the land, watching over Skell's borders whilst remaining largely undisturbed in their ancient and sacred woods.

This race of giants was known as Woodland Giants and was a stark contrast to their more volatile cousins, the Fire Giants of the southern volcanoes and the Frost Giants of the northern wastelands. Whilst the Woodland Giants were peaceful, wise, and content to live hidden deep within the Torreldane Woods, the Fire and Frost Giants roamed their respective lands with far greater aggression, looking for trouble.

"Giants!" Marcella shouted, the panic rising in her chest as she caught sight of the looming figures across the clearing.

The first strike came swiftly and brutally. A giant swung its club down, and the impact shattered the tranquillity of the forest, sending a shower of debris flying toward the Humans. "We need to fall back!" Marcella cried, her instincts screaming at her to escape as her men scrambled to avoid the crashing destruction of fallen trees and splintered branches.

The Dwarves, further north and unaware of the unfolding chaos, had just begun to notice the danger approaching. Despite the horror of the situation, they were not inclined to flee. Instead, they prepared to face the threat head-on.

Tholgar Ironfist gripped his Warhammer, his resolve solidifying into determination. “We’ve fought worse!” he roared, leading his men into a charge. They surged forward, aiming for the legs of the giants, their weapons striking with the ferocity characteristic of Dwarven warriors. The first blow landed with a resounding impact, causing one of the giants to stumble backwards, crashing to the ground with a thunderous boom.

As the giants charged with their enormous clubs raised high, their thunderous footfalls shook the very ground beneath the Dwarves’ feet. Tholgar Ironfist, at the head of his regiment, braced himself for the oncoming storm, but even he could not have predicted the sheer devastation that was about to unfold.

With one sweeping motion, the first of the giants brought its colossal club crashing down. The thick wooden weapon, studded with jagged iron spikes, tore through the Dwarven front line as though they were mere dolls. The impact was catastrophic. Warriors were sent flying into the air, their heavy armour offering little resistance to the immense force. Bodies collided with trees, rocks, and the earth, and their once-disciplined ranks shattered in a matter of moments.

Tholgar's heart pounded in his chest as he watched his men fall like leaves in a storm. "Hold the line!" he roared, his voice drowned out by the shrieks of his men and the bellowing laughter of the giants. But it was no use. Each swing of the giants' clubs felled dozens of Dwarves at once, their limbs crushed, their weapons scattered to the wind. The sound of metal meeting flesh echoed through the battlefield, a cacophony of death and destruction.

Another giant swung wide, and Tholgar barely had time to leap aside as a massive club smashed into the ground where he had been standing. The force of the blow sent a shockwave through the earth, knocking more of them off their feet. One warrior, caught directly in the swing, was lifted clear off the ground, his body flung into a nearby tree with a sickening crunch.

"By the gods..." Brokk Stonebeard muttered, his axe raised as he watched his comrades torn apart. His face was pale, eyes wide with horror at the overwhelming might of the giants.

"They're too strong!" one of the younger Dwarves shouted, his voice cracking with panic. "We can't—!"

Tholgar cut him off with a bellow. "We fight, or we die! Aim for their legs; bring them down!" Desperation laced his voice, but he refused to give in to the terror that gnawed at his insides. This was not how it was supposed to go. They were Dwarves—proud, relentless, undefeated in countless wars. Yet here they were, being slaughtered like animals.

Several men took his command to heart, charging forward and targeting the giants' thick legs with their axes and hammers. The brave soldiers of Hammerdeep struck with all their might, aiming for the knees and ankles, hoping to cripple the massive foes. One giant faltered, letting out a deep, guttural howl as a well-aimed hammer crushed its knee. The enormous beast collapsed, its fall sending a tremor through the ground.

For a fleeting moment, hope surged through the Dwarven ranks. But as the giant fell, three more took its place, their massive forms blotting out the sky as they swung their clubs with savage glee. A single swipe from one giant sent a dozen Dwarves sprawling, their bones shattered, blood spraying in a grotesque arc.

"Fall back!" Tholgar shouted, his voice hoarse. His heart sank as he saw more and more of his men crumple under the might of the giants. The ground beneath them was soaked with Dwarven blood, the rich, dark soil now a crimson quagmire.

Another giant slammed its club into the earth, narrowly missing Brokk, who had barely managed to roll out of the way. "Tholgar!" he gasped, scrambling to his feet. "We can't hold them! We've got to retreat!"

Tholgar gritted his teeth, hatred, and fury boiling inside him. He wanted nothing more than to stand

and fight, to drive his hammer into the heart of every giant until the land was free of their monstrous presence. But the truth was undeniable—they were outmatched.

"Retreat!" Tholgar finally shouted, his voice carrying above the din of battle. "Get the wounded and fall back! We regroup at the shore!"

The Dwarves, their spirits shattered, but their will to survive, stronger than their pride, began to retreat. They dragged their injured comrades with them, forming a desperate, disorganised line as they fled the battlefield. Behind them, the giants roared in triumph, their thunderous voices shaking the very trees as they watched the Dwarves scramble for their lives.

As the fallen soldiers of Hammerdeep retreated, the echoes of the battle continued to haunt them. They could still hear the crack of bones, the crash of clubs, the screams of their fallen brothers. But there was no time to mourn, no time to reflect on their defeat. They had to return to Hammerdeep, regroup, and prepare for what would come next.

Tholgar, his armour battered and slick with blood, led the retreat. His warhammer, once shining with the pride of Dwarven craftsmanship, was now caked with dirt and gore. His eyes burned with the promise of vengeance, his mind already turning towards their next assault.

As they neared their boat, Tholgar cast one last look over his shoulder at the battlefield they had left behind. The giants, still towering and triumphant, watched them retreat with smug satisfaction. But this was not the end. It was merely the beginning.

“We’ll be back,” Tholgar growled under his breath, “And when we return, we’ll bring hell with us.”

The retreat of the Dwarves was not one of cowardice but of necessity. His warriors, fewer than when they had first landed, stumbled behind him, dragging their wounded through the underbrush. They moved with grim determination, unwilling to speak of the failure that had befallen them. The Dwarven pride, so deeply ingrained in their culture, hung heavy in the air like an unspoken vow to return—stronger, fiercer.

As they neared the coastline, Tholgar turned to his second-in-command, Brokk Stonebeard, who limped beside him, his axe still slick with giant blood. “We can’t fight them like this,” Tholgar growled, his voice low but seething with frustration. “Those giants… they were unexpected.”

Brokk, with his bloodied face and eyes burning with the same stubborn fire that all his companions shared, nodded. “Aye, but we’ll not be beaten so easily. This is only a setback. Once we return to Hammerdeep, we’ll gather the War Elephants. The giants won’t stand a chance against the Dwarven Crossbows.”

Tholgar grunted in agreement, his mind already planning their next move. The Dwarves were a people known for their resilience and their unwillingness to admit defeat. Hammerdeep, their mountain fortress, was only a few days' journey by sea. Once there, they would regroup and return with their greatest weapon—the giant war elephants, each capable of carrying four to five warriors on its back, armed with mounted crossbows that could pierce even the toughest of giant hides.

As they boarded their ships, they moved in near silence, the weight of their losses settling over them like a shroud. The wind whipped at their faces as the boats cut through the waves, heading north towards the familiar, towering peaks of Hammerdeep. Tholgar stood at the prow of the lead ship, his eyes locked on the distant horizon. He could still hear the echoes of battle in his mind—the clash of steel, the thunderous fall of the giants, and the screams of his fallen comrades.

"Tholgar," Brokk said quietly, joining him at the front of the ship. "What will we do when we return?"

Tholgar's jaw clenched, his gaze never wavering from the mountains ahead. "We prepare for war," he said, his voice cold and resolute. "The giants may have the land for now, but they won't for long. Not once we bring out the war elephants."

Brokk's eyes gleamed at the thought. The war elephants of Hammerdeep were legendary, massive beasts bred in the highlands, armoured in thick steel, and capable of carrying entire squads of Dwarven crossbowmen on their backs. With their size and power, they could charge through the thickest ranks of enemies and turn the tide of any battle.

“Aye,” Brokk said, a grin forming beneath his thick beard. “The giants won’t know what hit them.”

Tholgar allowed himself a rare smile, though it was tinged with bitterness. “We’ll hit them hard, but we’ll need more than just brute force. We need to be smarter and faster. The elves are waiting, too, and they’ll be ready for us.”

As the sea grew calmer, the conversation continued. They discussed the strategy for their next assault, their voices low so as not to stir the men, who needed rest after the brutal retreat.

“We can’t just rely on the elephants,” Brokk added, his face puzzled in thought. “The elves have archers, and their magic can turn the tide. We need to strike before they’re ready.”

Tholgar nodded, his eyes narrowing. “Brokk, they have no magic. We’ll bring our entire nation. Every warrior will follow us into battle.”

Brokk grunted his approval. “And once we’re through, we’ll head straight for the elven city. They’re the ones pulling the strings here. Take out their leadership, and the giants will fall with them.”

The two Dwarves stood in silence for a moment, watching the sun dip lower into the ocean.

The thought of revenge burned in their hearts, and so did the desire to recoup and return to their homeland. Hammerdeep was more than just a fortress; it was the heart of their people.

"We'll need every man we have," Tholgar finally said, breaking the silence. "Every warrior, every smith. Hammerdeep will go to war."

Brokk nodded solemnly. "And when we return, we won't be retreating again."

As the coastline of Hammerdeep came into view, the Dwarves began to stir, their tired eyes lighting up at the sight of home. The great mountain fortress rose high into the sky, its stone walls and towers blending seamlessly with the rocky cliffs. Inside those walls, an inspired army of Hammerdeep would prepare. The forges would burn hot, the war elephants would be armoured, and the giant crossbows would be mounted with the huge steel arrows sharp and in the supply of plenty.

Tholgar turned to his men, his voice rising above the sound of the crashing waves. "Rest whilst you can, lads. Once we set foot on Hammerdeep's soil, we prepare for war."

And so, the Dwarves sailed into the shadow of their mighty fortress, their hearts heavy with loss but burning with the promise of vengeance. The giants had won this battle, but the war was far from over.

As the Humans regrouped, their hearts heavy with the weight of their near defeat, Marcella and her companions shared frantic glances. They had survived the initial onslaught, but the terror of the giants loomed large in their minds. "What do we do now?" one of her fellow soldiers asked, his voice trembling.

"We need to rethink our strategy," Marcella replied, her mind racing. "We cannot allow ourselves to be caught off guard again. These giants are only one threat; we must uncover what other dangers lurk in this land."

King Cael said with intent, "Marcella, the giants serve the Elves; they did not act out of pure aggression; they served the Queen for many years with honour. The Queen was good to them, and she made the giants stronger with her magic; even though she is gone, the giants remain loyal to her and will defend the land from anyone." he paused to think and then continued, "We need shelter, a place to regroup and plan our next moves. We cannot let fear dictate our actions." His leadership shone through, rallying the hearts of the Humans and igniting a flicker of hope amidst their despair.

As they retreated towards the sea, they could see a glimpse of a small group of creatures a few miles north. At this point, King Cael had just realised he'd seen the Dwarves. With his mind racing, he kept this to himself to avoid causing mayhem and drama; he bellowed orders to his band of warriors to distract them.

The human forces marched back to their ships, the weight of their near defeat hanging heavy over them. The air was thick with the stench of battle and the distant roars of giants, which still echoed in their ears. King Cael led the retreat, his daughter Marcella by his side. They moved swiftly but not in panic—determined to regroup, not to flee.

The rhythmic crashing of the waves became louder as they neared the shore, their boats in sight. But the journey home would not be one of relief. The human soldiers, bloodied and battered, exchanged weary glances, their shoulders slumped with exhaustion. Some whispered nervously among themselves whilst others remained silent, lost in their thoughts.

One of Marcella's fellow soldiers, his voice trembling, broke the silence: "What do we do now, Marcella? We barely survived this. Those giants... They're more powerful than anything we've faced."

Marcella, her sharp eyes scanning the horizon, tried to steady her breath. "We need to rethink everything," she replied, her tone serious but composed. "We can't afford another ambush like that. The giants are just one threat, but who knows what else is out there? We must return, regroup, and come back prepared."

King Cael overheard their exchange and nodded in agreement, his expression stern but resolute. "She's right. Fear will only weaken us. We must be strategic now more than ever. We need shelter, time to plan, and more men." His voice carried strength, a rallying force that sparked a flicker of hope in the hearts of his soldiers.

Marcella turned to her father, speaking more quietly now. "We can't go back like this, Father. The men are disheartened. The elves are stronger than we anticipated. The giants are an unexpected force. We need more than just tactics. We need reinforcements."

Cael glanced around, ensuring the rest of the soldiers were focused on their retreat. His mind raced, recalling the glimpse of Dwarves he had seen earlier, a few miles north. They, too, had faced the elves and their giant allies. Perhaps there was an opportunity here, but now was not the time to reveal it.

"We will return with more men, Marcella," said the King, his voice low. "But we need to think bigger. The giants are powerful, but they aren't invincible. We'll need siege weapons, armour for the horses, and far more than what we have now. We cannot just meet them in open battle."

She nodded in agreement. "We need to strike where they least expect it. The mainland is vast, so we must find weak points. But first, we need to convince the nobles back home to raise more soldiers. It's not going to be easy."

Cael let out a heavy breath. "No, it won't. We'll have to show them the threat. They'll need to see the devastation firsthand and hear the stories of those who barely survived. We'll gather them in the capital—show them the scars of battle and the terror we faced."

Marcella looked out over the sea as the first boat reached the water. "And what of the Elves, Father? They'll be stronger next time. More prepared."

Cael's brow furrowed, his eyes darkening with thought. "We won't face them alone next time." He hesitated briefly, his thoughts returning to the small band of dwarves he had seen. "There may be others on this mainland who seek revenge as much as we do. But we need to approach them carefully—alliances are fragile, and everyone is out for their gain."

Marcella caught the shift in his tone but didn't press him further. There would be time for those discussions later. For now, they needed to get home safely.

As they reached the chilly waters of the shoreline, the sounds of the waves tumbling started drowning out the victorious roars of the giants; this was comforting to hear for the humans, who were still ripe with fear and adrenaline. The soldiers began boarding the boats; Cael took one last look over his shoulder at the distant land of Skell, now barely visible in the setting sun. The air was still thick with the tension of battle, and he could almost feel the eyes of the giants watching them from the mountains.

"We'll return," the King muttered under his breath. "We know what we face now; we now have the advantage of surprise."

Marcella, standing by his side, nodded in agreement. "We will, Father. And when we do, the elves will know fear as we have."

She walked along the boat's deck, trying to keep her balance as it dipped side to side, slowly riding the rhythm of the sea. Intrusive thoughts started racing around her brain; she was riddled with anxiety as she remembered how viciously the pterodactyls attacked them on their way to Skell.

Nervously, she chuckled to herself and exclaimed in a light-hearted manner, "Well, at least if we get attacked by the flying monsters again, we will have won two battles today and lost one, not a bad first day."

A few cheap laughs erupted from the men.

King Cael furiously turned around, shouting, "Marcella." Silence spread among the crew before the King took a deep breath before calmly but firmly continuing, "Now is not the time for jokes; we've lost good men today; we shall not disrespect them; they died for nothing."

Defensively, Marcella responded, "Well, I was just saying we know we can fight off the birds if they come back."

Her father turned to the captain of the boat and ordered, “Do a head count and get the crew ready to set sail; the sooner we are home, the better. I need rest...and time to think.”

The ships pushed off from the shore, sails catching the evening wind. As the coastline of Skell slowly disappeared behind them, the humans knew they had no choice but to regroup, to build a force stronger than ever before. The next time they set foot on that cursed land, it would not be to retreat. It would be to conquer.

As the waves carried them back to their island, King Cael turned to Marcella, his eyes heavy but determined. “We will need every advantage, every ally we can muster. The next move is ours. We've seen their strength; we were merely a band of scouts, and we have the element of surprise in terms of our strength... and, also, Marcella, please, for both our sakes, I need you to watch what you say in front of the men, you are the princess, your words don't fall on deaf ears.”

Marcella met his gaze, her eyes filled with an apologetic resolve. “I'm sorry for letting you down; I was just trying to be in high spirits in front of the crew and boost morale.”

“It's okay, my daughter, her father replied in an understanding manner, “You are still learning; just remember who you are before you speak and try to play the jester.”

Meanwhile, Tholgar Ironfist and the remaining Dwarves also regrouped, though the atmosphere among them was far grimmer. They had underestimated the giants and their overwhelming strength. The blood of their fallen comrades weighed heavily on their hearts, and whispers of doubt began to circulate among the ranks. “We should’ve stayed away from this cursed place,” one of the younger Dwarves muttered.

Tholgar silenced him with a fierce glare. “Do not speak such words! We are Dwarves; we stand and fight. We will find a way to drive these giants back or die trying!” His fervour ignited a spark of resolve in his men, though the fear of the giants lingered like a spectre over them.

Both factions were now embroiled in their battles, facing not just the threats of Skell but also the weight of their history, their animosities, and the realisation that survival would demand more than mere strength. The island was a complex tapestry of beauty and peril, and as the sun finally dipped below the horizon, the darkness revealed yet another layer of Skell’s enigmatic nature—a world filled with wonders and horrors waiting to be uncovered.

The paths of the Humans and Dwarves, though miles apart, were now intricately linked by the shared experience of danger. Neither was aware that their fates would soon intertwine in ways they could never foresee as the true heart of Skell began to reveal itself, shrouded in shadows and ancient secrets.

Whilst the other factions battled giants in the south, the snowpeople approached from the north. Their arctic ship glided silently through the icy waters, and as they stepped onto the frosted snow banks, the landscape shifted into a wintery wonderland.

As the darkness of night snuck into the sky and the moon was bright, casting a silvery glow across the frozen landscape, High Priestess Ylvana stood among the snowpeople, a fierce pride swelling within her. Their breaths plumed in the crisp air, mingling with the soft crunch of snow beneath their feet. Frost Giants lay defeated, their massive bodies sprawled across the white canvas like shattered statues of a long-lost age. Ice crystals sparkled around them, glistening in the fading light—a stark reminder of the ferocity with which the snowpeople had reclaimed their territory.

The battle had been swift and brutal. Ylvana had felt the shift in the winds, the ominous approach of the Frost Giants, their ancient forms looming like dark clouds against the horizon. The snowpeople, long exiled and weary, had gathered under her guidance, fueled by the anger and sorrow of generations past. They had sworn to reclaim their land, a promise made under the watchful eyes of their ancestors.

As the Giants marched, Ylvana gathered the clans. With her silver hair flowing like a waterfall of snow, she addressed them: "We are not mere survivors; we are warriors of the ice. We will strike before they reach our homes and before they plunge us back into darkness. Together, we will harness the spirit of our ancestors." The beasts of Jotungard had moved like shadows across the tundra, their half-wolf forms blending seamlessly with the snow. Toric, their fierce commander, had led the charge, his howl echoing through the valleys, rallying his kin. With their hearts pounding in their chests, they prepared to confront the ancient foes that had hunted them for far too long.

As the giants approached, the ground trembled beneath their enormous feet, each step reverberating like thunder. The snowpeople, emboldened by their unity, flanked the giants, using the terrain to their advantage. The freezing wind howled, creating a natural cover as they launched their assault.

In the first clash, the snowpeople struck with a ferocity that surprised even themselves. They climbed the mountains of snow, utilising their agility to leap onto the backs of the giants, sinking their claws into the ice-cold flesh. Ylvana, standing at the heart of the fray, channelled the strength of her ancestors; she ran towards a huge boulder wedge in the snow and leapt off it, swinging her elven ice staff over her head towards a Giant's throat. She sliced through its thick and leathery skin with ease; the giant collapsed, clenching his throat whilst he slowly bled to death.

"Now!" she cried, her voice cutting through the roar of the winds. "Strike true!"

With that command, the wolf-like beings surged forward; their attacks synchronised like a well-rehearsed dance. Toric faced the largest giant, a behemoth whose icy breath could freeze a man in seconds. As the giant swung a massive fist, Toric ducked, rolling beneath the blow, then sprang upwards, his claws aimed for the giant's throat. He landed a deep gash, causing the creature to roar in pain.

But the fight was not without its challenges. The giants retaliated, swinging their colossal arms and unleashing blasts of freezing air that threatened to encase the snowpeople in ice. "Is that all they've got? Haha, they are pathetic; we don't bow to coldness; coldness bows to us" Ylvanas words were met with roars and howls from her warriors.

As the battle raged on, Ylvana moved like a spectre, weaving through the chaos. She conjured ice shards that shot toward the giants like arrows, striking their vulnerable joints and bringing them to their knees. The giants, once the lords of the land, were faltering under the relentless assault of the snowpeople.

Realising the tide was turning, the Frost Giants began to retreat, trying to regroup. But Toric saw their hesitation as an opportunity. "Push forward!" he shouted. "We cannot let them escape!"

With renewed vigour, the snowpeople pressed their attack, emboldened by the scent of victory. As the giants fell, one by one, their energy surged.

Each defeat was a release of years of pent-up anger and grief, the echoes of their ancestors fueling their strength.

At last, Ylvana stood before the final giant, a towering figure whose frostbitten eyes burned with rage. She faced him with unwavering resolve. “Your reign of terror ends here,” she declared, her voice steady.

The giant roared, ice forming around his fists as he charged. But Ylvana called upon the full force of her army with a final, coordinated strike; they collectively brought the giant crashing down, his massive form collapsing into the snow, a defeated titan. The field was silent now, the air heavy with the weight of their victory. The Frost Giants, once seen as invincible, lay vanquished, their icy breaths stilled.

High Priestess Ylvana surveyed the scene, her heart swelling with a mixture of triumph and sorrow. “We have reclaimed our land,” she said, her voice ringing clear. “Let this victory mark a new era for the snowpeople. We are no longer in exile; we stand united in our strength.”

The snowpeople erupted into cheers, their voices rising like a chorus of wolves under the moonlight. They had not only fought for their territory but had forged an unbreakable bond through the fires of battle. The shadows of the past began to fade, replaced by the shimmering hope of a brighter future.

As they gathered around the fallen giants, the air filled with the electricity of their triumph. Ylvana knew that this was only the beginning. The North had heard their howl, and they would not go back into the darkness. Together, they would build a new home, one where their families could thrive, free from the threats of the past.

With the stars twinkling above them and the chill of victory coursing through their veins, they prepared for the next chapter of their story, ready to reclaim not just their land but their rightful place in the world.

Toric sheathed his bloodied blade and looked out over the battlefield, his heart swelling with a mixture of pride and something darker—an insatiable thirst for vengeance. The snowpeople had lived in exile for far too long, and though their victory here was sweet, it was only the beginning. The frosty winds whispered promises of revenge against those who had wronged them, particularly the elves who had pushed them into the shadows.

He turned to his companions, their half-wolf, half-human forms bristling with energy and ferocity. "We've reclaimed our land in the north," he announced, his voice steady. "But this is not where our fight ends. The elves will pay for what they've done. We must march south, reclaim what was lost, and take back our honour."

High Priestess Ylvana seconded this, "Toric, you are right. The elves should pay the price for what they have done. I want you to take the night to rest and, by noon the next day, have an army ready to march south."

A murmur of unease rippled through the group. Though they had tasted victory, the thought of leaving their families behind in this newfound homeland was unsettling. They had toiled for generations to find a haven, a place they could call their own, after years of wandering and oppression.

One of the older warriors, Kalan, stepped forward, his expression grim. "Toric, we can't abandon our families. They've just begun to settle here, to find peace among the ice and snow. We should fortify this place and strengthen our hold before we consider venturing into the south."

Toric's jaw tightened. He understood the weight of Kalan's words; he felt it, too. But the fire of vengeance burned brightly in his chest, blinding him to the apprehension that clouded his companions' hearts. "Do you think the elves will give us the time to fortify? Whilst we sit idle, they will grow stronger, and we will be forgotten once more."

"But if we leave, we risk everything," Kalan insisted, his voice rising with the urgency of his plea. "Our children, our elders—they are vulnerable here. We can't just abandon them to fight a war that is not ours alone."

Toric shook his head, frustration simmering beneath his cool exterior. "It is ours. We are snowpeople, forged in the cold, bound by blood to the land of Skell. Our history is one of conflict, of standing against the tide. If we do not act now, we may never have another chance."

The tension in the air thickened, a tangible mix of determination and dread. Other warriors nodded in agreement with Kalan, their loyalty to their families evident in their expressions. But Toric felt the weight of leadership bearing down on him. He had always been the one to lead them through storms, to guide them back to the heart of their homeland. Yet now, he faced a battle not just against the elves but within his own ranks.

"We are a pack," Toric said, his voice dropping to a low growl. "And as a pack, we must make sacrifices. To reclaim our honour, we may have to leave behind those we love, if only for a time. This is our chance to carve a future for them, one where they will no longer live in fear. We can return for them once the elves are dealt with."

A heavy silence fell over the group as they considered his words. The battle they had just fought still echoed in their minds, a reminder of the strength they wielded together. But Toric's resolve to march south was a weighty burden. They had fought not just against the Frost Giants but against the memories of their past—a past steeped in loss and pain.

Finally, a voice spoke from the back. It was Marcella, a fierce warrior known for her sharp wit and keen senses. “If we do this, we must be smart about it. We can’t charge blindly into the south without a plan. The elves are cunning and powerful; they will not be caught off guard again.”

Toric nodded, appreciating her insight. “We’ll need to scout ahead and gather intelligence on their movements and their alliances. I don’t wish to leave our families unprotected, but the South holds the key to our future.”

“What if we send a small group to the south first?” suggested Kalan, his tone softer now, more conciliatory. “A scouting party will assess the situation whilst the rest of us stay behind. If things go poorly, we can regroup and fortify our defences here.”

Toric considered this for a moment. It was a compromise he could work with. “Very well. We will send a group to gather information. But they must move quickly and quietly. We can’t afford to lose the element of surprise, but we are leaving here by noon tomorrow at the command of the High Priestess Ylvana.”

The murmurs of agreement echoed around him, a small flicker of unity igniting amongst the snowpeople. They were not just warriors; they were a family bound by shared struggles and dreams. Toric felt a surge of gratitude for their loyalty, but the fire of vengeance still flickered within him. He would lead them into battle, one way or another.

With a plan forming, the warriors of Jotungard set to work. Some began to clear the battlefield, moving the fallen Frost Giants and securing their victory. Others scouted the perimeter, ensuring their newly claimed territory was safe from any lingering threats.

As the sun dipped lower, painting the sky with hues of lavender and deep blue, Toric gathered the chosen few for the scouting party. They stood at the edge of the frozen beach, the icy wind whipping around them. Marcella, Kalan, and a few other seasoned warriors stood ready, their faces set with determination.

"Remember," Toric said, "we are not just fighting for ourselves, but for the generations to come. This is for our families and every Snowperson who has suffered at the hands of the elves. We will return with knowledge and strength."

With that, they set off into the deepening dusk, shadows stretching behind them as they moved south. The moon rose high in the sky, casting an otherworldly glow over the snow-covered terrain. Toric felt the weight of his decisions, the burden of leadership heavy on his shoulders, yet there was a flicker of hope—an ember that promised that they could reclaim their rightful place in the world.

Back at the newly established settlement, the families of the snowpeople gathered around fires, their laughter echoing through the cold night air. Though the warriors had left, their spirit remained—a reminder that they were more than just a scattered group; they were a people with a shared destiny.

But as Toric advanced into the night, guided by the stars and the howl of the wind, he knew that the fight was far from over. The Frost Giants were only the beginning, and the true battle awaited them in the south. The echoes of the past would guide his blade, and he vowed to ensure that the snowpeople would rise again, unbroken and unyielding, beneath the icy skies of Skell.

Chapter Eleven

Deep in the forest, where the trees towered like great ancient beings themselves, one of the surviving giants, a scout named Tharl, knelt beside the crumbled remains of his fallen kin. His breath came in deep, thunderous huffs, his stone-like skin covered in dirt and blood. He had to move quickly.

The elven King needed to know what had happened on the Eastern shores. The giants, Queen Elaena's faithful servants, had always stood guard over Skell, ensuring the island remained hidden from the prying eyes of outsiders. But now that the factions had returned, the conflict would only grow more fierce. Tharl stood to his full height, towering above the treetops, and began his journey east towards the capital city. Every step he took left deep craters in the earth, shaking the ground like distant thunder.

The elven fortress atop the great Mount Morvem, known as Heaven Keep, was a marvel of architectural brilliance. From a distance, the castle shimmered like a beacon, its outer shell crafted entirely from precious stone, glistening under the sun. The towers spiralled elegantly into the sky, their surfaces imbued with shifting hues that reflected the changing light of day and night. The castle's turrets gleamed with a pearlescent glow, and its gates were lined with intricate carvings of ancient elven symbols, each one representing a forgotten tale from the distant past.

Inside this grand facade, however, lay a secret far more wondrous. The vast halls of the above-ground structure seemed deceptively simple in comparison to what was hidden below. The centrepiece of the grand hall was an ornate golden hatch—its doors made of pure gold. Runes were etched into its surface, swirling with the literature of magic that few could read. This hatch led to the true heart of the elven stronghold, an underground castle known only to the most powerful of the elven aristocracy. Only people who had been verbally invited by one of the elders could enter the bunker; you couldn't open the doors without consent; it was physically impossible.

Upon opening the golden doors, a grand spiral staircase descended deep into the masterpiece which had been carved out of the heart of the mountain. The staircase was wide and bordered by marble bannisters inlaid with gold and silver filigree. As one descended, the air itself seemed to shimmer with magic, growing heavier and more potent the deeper one went.

The underground fortress was a labyrinth of luxury and power, sprawling twenty levels deep, each floor a testament to the wealth and craftsmanship of the

Elves. The walls of the subterranean castle were constructed from the rarest materials found in the world. Gold veins ran through marble floors, and the ceilings were adorned with mosaics of precious gems that formed constellations, mythical creatures, and scenes of great elven victories.

Each floor was connected by delicate bridges made of glass, crystal, and silver, suspended over grand halls or flowing streams of vitamin-rich water that coursed through the fortress, providing both beauty and health for the habitants. In the time of Elaena, the water itself was said to be infused with magic, glowing faintly as it moved through the castle and sustaining the complex spells that protected the Kingdom.

The residents of this secretive underground world were elven nobles, scholars, and high-ranking officials. They strolled through the shimmering halls in garments that reflected their status—robes of deep crimson and violet, trimmed with silver and gold threads. Their cloaks seemed to float behind them, embroidered with symbols that signified their status and power. The fabric itself was enchanted, soft as silk but impenetrable to most mortal weapons, a subtle but ever-present reminder of their elevated status.

Every noble bore intricate jewellery—rings, necklaces, and masks—studded with rare gems that not only displayed their wealth but the image the snobbish race liked to portray of themselves to the rest of the world. These elves walked with an air of effortless grace, their gazes cool and calculated, discussing politics, the magical theory behind Elaena, and the ruling of the land in hushed tones as they crossed the many bridges that spanned the castle's inner courtyards and chambers.

At the centre of the castle's grand hall, a monumental wall stood, carved from the purest form of obsidian, veined with lines of silver. This wall, known as the Wall of Eternity, depicted the legend of Queen Elaena, whose rise to power changed the fate of the elven race. The carvings were a masterpiece of elven artistry; each figure was brought to life with such detail that they seemed to move when the flickering torchlight hit them just right.

At the top of the wall was Elaena herself, her face calm and serene, her eyes being represented by beautiful purple gemstones, glistening as they reflected the light of the surroundings. Below her, scenes from her life were chiselled in perfect detail—her discovery of magic during the reign of King Draegon, her powerful spell that lifted the veil of secrecy around their race, and the war she waged with her father, King Braegon Fikshire to reclaim the throne from human rule. The final panel had only just been finished; it showed her funeral, surrounded by her most loyal warriors, with her crown of flames burning brightly as she took her place as Queen of the people.

The elves considered this wall sacred. It wasn't just a tribute to Elaena but a source of inspiration and reverence for the elven people. Every inch of the Wall of Eternity seemed to still radiate magic; it was said that if one of another race touched the carvings, they would instantly set alight and burn to death, which had yet to be witnessed.

In other parts of the underground world, the walls of the hidden city were covered in intricate carvings that told the history of the Elves, stretching back to the creation of their race. Every archway was decorated with intertwined patterns of nature and elven runes —branches and leaves that seemed to move with the seasons, stars that twinkled in constellations, and animals carved from stone that seemed to occasionally shift positions when no one was looking.

Columns rose to impossible heights, each one sculpted from rare, shimmering stones—obsidian, jade, and quartz—catching the light and reflecting it in kaleidoscopic patterns across the halls. The air was filled with the faint hum of magic, an ever-present energy that flowed through the veins of the castle like blood. Floating lights hovered in mid-air, changing in intensity and colour depending on the time of day, casting everything in an ethereal glow.

Magical wards, both seen and unseen, still protected every level of the castle. The mountain itself powered these spells; nobody could figure out why this magic from Elaena remained; this was only because she never shared details of her most vital work. She had created an invisible chamber hidden in the very bones of the mountain. This secret room was concealed not by illusion alone but by the mountain itself, camouflaged by the natural stone and enchanted to reveal itself only to Elaena.

When Elaena stood before the wall, it would only respond to her whispered command. The stone seemed to ripple like water, the very rock melting away to reveal a hidden entrance. Beyond this, the small room appeared. In its centre sat a massive golden dish, sitting on top of a short, stumpy brass column. Branching off the column were what looked like the roots of a tree, but they were see-through and glowed purple, the same glow of Elaenas eyes radiating with power. The dish, intricately engraved with magical runes and elven symbols, contained the water from the river that flowed through the mountain.

The water alone didn't power the mountain; it was the two strange stones that floated within the dish, spinning endlessly in the magical currents. These stones, unlike anything seen before, had been crafted from five materials: stone from the mountain, obsidian, diamond, a lock of Elaenas' hair, and bark from the oldest tree in Torreldane woods. These components had been melded together through magic, creating stones that pulsed with raw, untamable energy.

At their core, each stone contained a powerful magnet, ensuring that they spun in perpetual motion within the enchanted waters. Their motion, combined with the properties of the mountain's water, generated an endless flow of power—enough to sustain the elven city within without the need for outside resources. Even without Elaena's presence, the chamber functioned; the magic had become self-sustaining, woven into the fabric of the mountain itself. Unfortunately, she didn't figure out how to keep her magic going on the outside of the mountain before she died; things would have been very different if she had.

High King Zelder liked to sit in his grand hall above ground. It was carved from ancient stone and depths of the mountain that had been woven into the architecture of the castle by elven skills. His golden hair, though flecked with grey, was still regal, and his blue eyes—the mark of the Fikshire bloodline—glowed in the dim light of the throne room. Around him, the advisors and generals of the elven army stood, their faces tense with the weight of war.

"Your Majesty," Tharl's rumbling voice echoed through the hall as he entered, his massive figure barely fitting inside the vaulted ceilings. He knelt before the King, his stone knees cracking the marble floor.

"What have you to report, Tharl?" Zelder asked, his voice calm but underlined with a dangerous edge.

"The scouts from the three of the four factions have invaded Skell. The Dwarves fought bravely, but their numbers were too few. They retreated, but I fear they will return. The Humans were cautious but fled before the might of our forces. Yet the snowpeople from the north still march—unrelenting as the winter storms they come from, they killed all Frost Giants but one."

Zelder knew of the snowpeople well, some of the story books he read as a kid were all about them, half-wolf, half-human, and their resilience in the cold was unmatched. If they reached the northern forests of Skell, they would spread like a plague.

"We must prepare," the elven King said, standing. His voice cut through the room like a blade. "The snowpeople are relentless, and their march from the Arctic will not be halted easily. But fire... fire is their weakness."

"Fire giants, Your Majesty?" one of the advisors of the Royal Council suggested cautiously. Zelder nodded. "Yes, summon them. The fire giants of the south will burn their way through the wolves. They cannot withstand the flames. But we must not stop there. Prepare an army to guard the keep on the eastern coast."

A general stepped forward, his hand over his heart in salute. "How many, my King?"

Zelder's eyes glinted with cold determination. "Send five hundred archers and two hundred foot soldiers. They are to defend the coast against any who attempt to set foot on our shores again. We shall crush these invaders before they can even think of forming an alliance."

"But the Dwarves and Humans—" one of the generals began to say.

"The Dwarves and Humans are foolish, but they are not our greatest threat. The snowpeople will feel our wrath first."

Chapter Twelve

In the south of Skell, where the air shimmered with heat and the earth cracked from the pressure of molten rivers, the Fire Giants lived within the heart of the volcanoes. Their skin burned like embers, and their eyes glowed with the eternal fire that coursed through their veins. Rarely did they leave their molten domains, for their power was the land's last line of defence. But when King Zelder's summons came, they answered.

From the largest of the volcanoes, Mount Harkoth emerged the first of the Fire Giants. Their leader, Kragor, a massive figure with a crown of burning horns and molten armour that dripped lava as he walked, stood at the mouth of the volcano, waiting for his kin to join him. Around him, the heat distorted the air, making the very landscape seem to ripple. Kragor raised his hand, flames dancing from his fingertips as more of his kind emerged, their roars shaking the mountains. Together, they would form an unstoppable force of flame, turning the snowy north into ash and cinders.

As the elven army prepared, news of the Dwarves and Humans landing on the shores of the mainland spread quickly. Across the eastern coasts, elven soldiers began fortifying the keep, sharpening their arrows, and ensuring their armour was polished and strong. Their bows were strung, and their swords gleamed in the light of the fading sun.

At the command of General Laerion, the elven forces readied themselves. General Laerion gathered his men round for a speech.

“The enemies are injured and in retreat; we are here to make sure if they come back, we finish them off and defend our land; as soon they will land, they will descend upon us; we must be ready and ruthless,” Laerion said to his commanders. “We cannot let them advance into our lands. But our archers will hold them at bay from the keep. The Fire Giants will crush the enemies of the north, our job is to defend Selthor shore until given further instructions.”

An archer, his face pale with fear, spoke up. “But what of the other faction, General? The Orks—”

“They are not our concern. We have not received word on them yet. What we do know is that we have two enemy armies on Selthor shore, and north, we have the half-wolf, half-man horde of savages. Let’s stick to the facts for now.”

“Understood, sir,” the archer responded.

Chapter Thirteen

Unknown to the High Priestess Ylvana, an army of Fire Giants was steadily advancing north, closing the gap between the two opposing forces. These titanic beings, fierce and full of wrath, were led by their formidable leader, Kragor. The air thickened with heat as they marched forward, and the oppressive warmth they carried with them caused the once-frigid atmosphere to ripple with anticipation. Kragor, standing at the front of his army, was a towering figure of molten fury. His fiery armour blazed in the dim light, casting waves of heat that distorted the very air around him. His molten skin radiated a hellish glow, making the ground beneath his feet crack and hiss.

Kragor looked out over the distance and spotted the massive army of snowpeople ahead, their silvery forms reflecting the icy landscape. They appeared as cold and savage as ever, but he knew better. He knew that after their victory over the Frost Giants, they had grown too comfortable, too complacent. The snowpeople had become overconfident in their strength, thinking themselves untouchable. But Kragor would soon show them how misguided that arrogance was. The power of fire was eternal, and he would teach them that their fleeting victory meant nothing against the unyielding fury of flame.

As dawn began to break, the first rays of sunlight piercing through the clouds, a tremendous roar echoed from the Fire Giant ranks. Kragor's warriors were ready. Without warning, the Fire Giants launched their attack. Massive, flaming projectiles arced through the sky, trailing smoke and fire. The missiles landed with devastating force, setting the snow-covered fields ablaze. The snowpeople, taken completely by surprise, turned in horror towards the source of the destruction. What they saw chilled even their icy hearts.

A wave of Fire Giants, towering and fearsome, advanced on them with terrifying purpose. The earth itself trembled beneath the fiery giants' feet as they approached, their molten forms casting long shadows over the battlefield. At the head of the fiery horde was Kragor, his molten armour shining like a beacon of destruction. His crown of flame illuminated the sky, which had turned dark under the smoke and ash from the burning fields. Kragor's voice boomed across the battlefield, echoing like the rumble of a volcano. "We will show these frost-bitten fiends the true strength of fire!" he bellowed, the force of his words rolling across the battlefield like thunder.

The clash of the two armies was immediate and brutal. As the Fire Giants charged, their enormous, fiery bodies collided with the icy defences of the snowpeople. A roar erupted as the Fire Giants unleashed a terrifying breath of dragon-like fire upon the snowpeople. Great jets of flame scorched the ground, melting snow and turning the battlefield into a molten wasteland. The snowpeople, once full of confidence, were now utterly defenceless against this onslaught. Fire was their weakness, and as the flames engulfed them, their courage, their arrogance, and their bravery quickly evaporated in the face of overwhelming heat and destruction.

"Pathetic," Kragor growled, his voice a deep rumble that seemed to shake the air around him. He smashed his fist into the frozen ground, and the impact sent shockwaves rippling through the enemy ranks, shattering several of them into a spray of icy shards. "This is what they call an army? These brittle wretches dared to oppose me?"

His molten gaze followed one of his giants as it tore through a cluster of Snowpeople attempting to regroup. The massive creature swung its molten arms in wide arcs, each movement a blur of liquid fire and unrelenting power. Snowpeople melted and shattered with every swing; their desperate cries drowned out by the roar of the flames.

The frozen earth, once a pristine blanket of white, was now a scorched landscape of flame and ash. The snowpeople fought valiantly, but it was clear they stood no chance. One by one, they began to falter. Their once-glistening fur, shimmering with the beauty of ice and snow, became ashen and brittle under the relentless heat. Their defence, which had seemed so formidable just days before, crumbled under the weight of the Fire Giants' assault. The air was thick with the sound of crackling flames and the cries of the dying. General Toric looked around the battlefield in disbelief; his army obliterated almost within minutes, and he knew they'd lost. "RETREAT! SAVE YOURSELVES!" he screamed. One by one, the snowpeople began to turn and flee; their retreat was a glorious sight to the Fire Giants. Their once-glistening forms became burnt and wounded figures in the distance as they ran for their lives and brittle under the relentless assault. The Fire Giants roared in triumph, revelling in the crackling flames that consumed their foes.

The Fire Giants, fueled by their triumph, roared in victory as the snowpeople fell around them. Kragor, towering over the battlefield, raised his molten arms to the sky in triumph. His voice echoed once more, this time filled with the satisfaction of a warrior who had won a hard-fought victory. "Let this day be remembered as the day fire conquered ice!" he bellowed, his fiery crown blazing against the darkened sky. "Let them know that the warmth of our hearts shall never be extinguished!"

As the last of the snowpeople crumbled into ash, their icy forms melting into nothingness, the Fire Giants stood victorious amid the remains of their enemies. The snowfields, once pristine and white, had been transformed into a desolate wasteland of fire and molten earth. The once beautiful frozen landscape was now a charred testament to the power of the Fire Giants and their unrelenting fury.

With their victory complete, Kragor turned to his men and declared, "You must begin the march back to Mount Harkoth; our lands are defenceless without us. I will make my way to Ardenviel before joining you; I need to tell King Zelder of our success." They had fought with honour and ferocity, and they had avenged the wrongs done to them. The North, once a battleground of fire and ice, was now at peace, though the cost had been great. Kragor and his Fire Giants would now reign over the ashes of their fallen enemies, their hearts burning with pride as they honoured the memory of their late elven Queen, Elaena, who had once ruled these lands with grace and wisdom.

General Toric of the snowpeople led his battered and beleaguered army on a long and sorrowful march home. The retreat had begun in desperation, and what followed was a grim and gruelling journey through the frozen wilderness. Toric, who had once commanded a force of thousands, now found himself at the head of a fractured remnant of his proud army. The battle against the Fire Giants had left them devastated. Those who had survived the initial onslaught were broken in both body and spirit. Their once proud general, ashamed and heartbroken.

The snowpeople trudged across the icy tundra, their heavy limbs leaving deep prints in the snow,

now dragging with exhaustion. Many of those who had managed to flee the battlefield had not survived the journey. Some had succumbed to their injuries, their charred limbs unable to withstand the relentless cold. Others had been claimed by exhaustion, their energy drained by the brutal march, their bodies collapsing into the snow, where they were quickly swallowed by the frozen earth. The endless expanse of white stretched before them, an unforgiving reminder of their defeat.

Of the thousands who had once marched with Toric, fewer than one hundred remained. These survivors were all that was left of the once-proud army that had set out with the belief that nothing could stand in their way. Now, every step forward was a struggle. The cold, once a source of comfort and power for the snowpeople, now felt like an oppressive weight that sought to pull them into the icy depths of the north.

General Toric, though wounded, remained physically strong. His heart ached for the soldiers who had fallen, but he knew they had to reach home. As the general, he took responsibility for their defeat and silently vowed to ensure the survival of those who remained. He had led them into the heart of battle, believing they could overcome any foe.

“Toric,” Ylvana called, her voice carrying over the white ground with a commanding clarity. “What news do you bring?”

The general stopped before her, his head bowed low. "High Priestess," he began, his voice hoarse. "We failed. The Fire Giants...they were unlike anything we've ever faced. They burned through our ranks like dry grass in a summer blaze.."

Ylvana's expression remained unreadable as she looked at the ragged group behind him. "This is all that remains of our army?"

Toric nodded, his shoulders slumping. "Aye. Many didn't survive the retreat."

Ylvana's sharp eyes softened ever so slightly, "You brought them home, Toric. That is more than I expected when I saw the flames rising in the south. We should never have challenged fire wielders."

Toric looked up at her, his face etched with regret. "It is not enough. I led them into ruin. I thought...I thought we could be smart about it. I thought—"

"Enough," Ylvana interrupted, her tone cold yet not unkind. "The blame does not lie solely with you. We were all naive to the truth of what fire can do to ice. You fought for our people. That is what matters now."

She turned to the soldiers, her voice rising. "You have endured the unendurable. You have survived the wrath of the Fire Giants, and you have returned to your home. That is no small feat. Rest now; recover your strength. You are the living heart of our people."

The soldiers nodded weakly, their relief palpable. Ylvana gestured to attendants nearby, who began helping the wounded inside the stronghold. She turned back to Toric, “Walk with me.”

The two moved through the gates and into the trees nearby, the icy branches shimmering faintly in the dim light. Once they were alone, Ylvana stopped and faced him. “The Fire Giants have shown us our vulnerability. To pursue vengeance would be nothing short of stupidity.”

Toric hesitated before speaking, his voice heavy with guilt. “What would you have us do, High Priestess? If we do not fight back, the rest will see us as weak.”

Ylvana’s eyes burned with anger. “Weak? We can take any faction apart from fire wielders; we are far from weak; do not insult me again!”

“I’m sorry, I meant no-”

“The north is ours by blood, by the spirits that dwell here. We do not need to prove our strength to anyone. We will rebuild, fortify, and grow stronger. This defeat has taught us that survival is not won through pride but through resilience. We can stop up here unchallenged, and we can rebuild.”

Toric frowned. “And the Fire Giants? They’ll come again. Perhaps not today, but someday.”

Ylvana's lips curled into a slight, determined smile. "They won't. We will harness the power of this land to build walls that even fire cannot breach. They have no reason to come back here; it's so far away from the south of the Island."

Toric bowed his head. "As you say, High Priestess. What are your orders?"

"Gather those who are fit, those still able to work. We will begin fortifying our new lands immediately. Dig into the ground, deepen our foundations, we will have a mighty stronghold, and ensure that no enemy can breach our walls. You will oversee the planning and construction. This is your penance, Toric—not to avenge, but to protect."

The general nodded solemnly. "I understand."

Ylvana placed a hand on his shoulder, her touch surprisingly warm. "Do not carry the weight of this loss alone. It is a burden we all share. Go now. Rest for tonight. Tomorrow, we begin."

As Toric departed, Ylvana turned back toward the hall, her expression cold like her surroundings. The loss weighed heavily on her, but she would not let it crush her. The snowpeople had suffered a great blow, but she would see to it that they rose from it stronger than ever. The north was their new home, and she would ensure it remained theirs—no matter the cost.

Chapter Fourteen

Meanwhile, on Gruk'Thor, the island south of Skell, the orks moved with purpose. Grugor, the ork chieftain, stood atop a platform in the centre of Gorthak, the great ork city. Towering stone walls surrounded the encampment, protecting it from the rough seas and the dense jungles beyond. The sound of hammers pounding on anvils echoed across the island as blacksmiths forged weapons for the coming battle.

Grugor's voice boomed over his warriors. "We go to war again! But this time, we do not run. We do not retreat. We will conquer the mainland and crush the elves beneath our boots!"

The Orks, known for their sheer strength and brutal efficiency, had assembled an army of 10,000 warriors. Their weapons were large, crude, and devastating: massive axes, spiked maces, and jagged swords forged from the iron-rich veins of their island's volcanic mountains.

In addition to their heavy infantry, the Orks unleashed their war machines—huge siege engines made from wood and reinforced metal, capable of tearing down the strongest fortifications. Their beasts of war, giant tusked boars, were saddled and armoured, ready to charge into battle with reckless abandon. They had managed to breed over 200 giant war boars, 6ft tall, weighing 900 lbs; these vicious creatures were not only the ork's favourite means of land transport but were also a great weapon when needed. Grugor raised his war axe, the blade gleaming in the sunlight. "To the volcanoes, through the jungle, and onto Ardenviel! To the land of Skell! And to victory!"

The Orks roared in unison as their fleet of ironclad ships set sail towards the mainland, preparing to traverse the fiery landscape of the southern volcanoes.

On Hammerdeep, the preparations were equally intense. Deep beneath the mountains of Grimstone, the Dwarves forged weapons and armour with precision unmatched by any other race. Their leader, King Tholgar Ironfist, stood at the heart of the great forge, surrounded by sparks and molten metal.

"Our kin fell to the giants, but we are not defeated!" Thrain bellowed. "We are Dwarves! Masters of stone, iron, and fire. Our hammers will ring loud in the halls of Skell, and the elves will fall before our might!"

The Dwarven army, 1,000-strong, was a disciplined and formidable force. They wielded masterfully crafted weapons—axes with razor-sharp edges, hammers capable of shattering bones, and shields that could deflect even the strongest blows. Their heavy armour, forged from the hardest steel, made them nearly impervious to normal weapons.

But their true strength lay in their war machines. Catapults and ballistae, designed to launch massive stones and spears, were readied for transport. Alongside them marched the Dwarven Ironbreakers—elite soldiers wielding massive hammers and shields, forming an impenetrable wall of iron.

The final and perhaps most formidable component of their army is the war elephants. They had 6 in total. These colossal creatures, adorned from head to tail with ancient Dwarven symbols painted in vibrant colours, are a sight to behold. Each elephant is clad in heavy Dwarven-forged armour and equipped with a fully automatic crossbow capable of holding up to 1,000 arrows at once.

The vessel carrying the elephants was a marvel of dwarven engineering, a colossal ship known as the Ironclad Titan. Crafted deep within the dwarven mountains, the ship had been the result of years of meticulous planning and construction. The dwarves had begun designing this ship decades ago, long before the war had reached the scale it did, anticipating a need for transporting the massive war elephants. It had waited patiently, dormant inside the hangars carved from the rock, ready for the day it would be called to action.

The Ironclad Titan was a behemoth unlike anything else on the seas. Its hull stretched over 500 feet long, constructed from layers of thick, iron-reinforced timber, enchanted with ancient runes to resist both the crushing weight of the elephants and the battering of enemy fire. The hull had the gleam of tempered steel, with rivets the size of a dwarf's fist, each one pounded into place with care. This reinforced structure gave the ship immense stability, ensuring that even when the elephants shifted their weight, the vessel would hold firm against the tumultuous seas.

The upper deck was broad and open, lined with rows of iron beams that were set deep into the hull for extra support. These beams were positioned to create platforms where the elephants could be securely stationed. Each platform had massive harnesses made of woven iron chains and thick leather straps. The deck had enough room to carry not only the elephants but also supplies for the journey, and a contingent of dwarven soldiers were tasked with maintaining the ship and caring for the animals.

The Ironclad Titan was powered by enormous paddles, which were turned by a complex system of gears and dwarf-powered cranks below deck. These paddles, reinforced with steel, cut through the water with surprising speed, given the ship's bulk. A sail made of Stomatosuchus hide, rare and nearly indestructible, was used to harness the wind when conditions allowed, but the dwarves relied more on the strength of their mechanical innovations.

For nearly thirty years, the Titan had been developed, refined, and perfected, with teams of dwarven engineers constantly working on improving its durability and seaworthiness. The dwarves had anticipated the need for a ship that could carry their giant beasts of war. The vessel had remained hidden in the mountain hangars for years,

King Tholgar Ironfist turned to his council and stated, “We sail at dawn. Let the elves try to stop us; they will taste the fury of Dwarven steel.”

The Dwarven fleet set sail, sturdy stone-hulled ships cutting through the waves as they approached the eastern coast of Skell.

On the human Island of Blackhaven, preparations took a different form. Princess Marcella had returned from her mission with her head down, they had been absolutely ripped apart and needed significantly more people to go on the next one. King Cael Emberfall stood atop the walls of his capital city, overlooking the bustling streets below. His army was assembling, and their tactics were already being drawn. Unlike the Orks’ brute strength or the Dwarves’ mechanical prowess, the Humans relied on strategy and precision.

“Prepare the men!” Cael commanded. “We face a strong enemy, but we do not face them alone.

Let our resolve be as strong as our steel and our tactics sharper than their arrows."

The human army was diverse and well-trained. Swordsmen, archers, and cavalry gathered in the city square, their armour gleaming in the sunlight. The Humans' strength lay in their adaptability, and they had prepared a mix of ranged and melee units to handle any situation. Their archers, skilled with longbows, could rain arrows on their foes from afar, whilst their knights and foot soldiers could form defensive lines or charge into battle.

Alongside them, the Humans brought packs of highly trained attack k9 units. King Cael himself donned his armour, a finely crafted set of plate mail, and mounted his warhorse.

"To Skell," he declared. "For honour, for our people, and our future."

After weeks of preparation, the time for war had come. Each faction, with its army of at least 1,000 warriors strong, set sail for Skell, determined to reclaim what was once theirs.

The Orks arrived first, their iron ships cutting through the dark seas as they approached the volcanic shores of the southern coast. The jagged peaks of Skell's volcanoes loomed in the distance, spewing ash and fire into the sky. As the Orks disembarked, they began their long march through the treacherous terrain of molten rock and lava flows. Their war machines, designed to handle the heat, creaked and groaned as they were dragged across the blackened earth. The Orks had a long way to go; given they were at the south shore after the Mountains, they still had miles of Jungle and then fields to cross before they would even be able to see the Capital city of Skell.

Meanwhile, the Dwarves and Humans arrived on the eastern coast, a few miles apart. The Dwarven fleet landed near the craggy cliffs, their soldiers immediately setting up fortifications and scouting the terrain. The Humans, not far to the south, landed on a sandy beach and began their preparations.

Word of the Dwarves and Humans' landings reached King Zelder quickly. However the Orks had gone unnoticed as the Fire Giants were still miles north after going to war with the Snow people from his throne, he summoned his most trusted generals.

"They've come as we knew they would," Zelder said coldly, his eyes glinting with determination. "But they are divided. We will split our forces to meet them—two armies to the east."

He raised his hand, issuing the command. "Send 500 more soldiers to both the eastern fronts. They will bolster our archers and foot soldiers already there. We must not let the Humans or Dwarves gain any ground. As for the Orks... the fire giants will deal with them if they decide they want to set foot on the mainland."

General Laerion nodded and began issuing orders. Elven troops, 500 archers, and 200-foot soldiers on each front moved swiftly along the eastern coastline to intercept the invaders. Another 1,000 soldiers followed, marching with precision and purpose to reinforce their comrades. The elves knew the terrain well and intended to use the dense forests and high cliffs to their advantage.

In the south, the Orks continued their advance through the volcanic landscape, the air thick with sulfur and the ground trembling with every eruption. Their war drums pounded, echoing off the mountain walls, as Grugor led the charge."Keep moving!" Grugor shouted, waving his axe in the air. "We are nearly at the Jungle, and then we bring war to the Elves!"

Back on the eastern shores, the Dwarves and Humans separately prepared for battle. King Tholgar Ironfist marched at the front of his army, his hammer raised high. "We make camp here, and tomorrow, we march into the heart of Skell! The elves will regret the day they banished us!"

Not far from the Dwarven camp, the Humans were doing the same. King stood atop a hill, watching the horizon. He knew the elves would not sit idly by whilst they advanced. And he was right.

As night fell, the first arrows flew through the air, marking the beginning of the battle. Elven archers, hidden in the treeline, rained death upon the human and Dwarven camps. King Tholgar unsheathed his sword, his voice steady as he called out, "Prepare for battle! The elves have come!"

Thousands of Dwarves were quickly finding cover as they saw the flashes of elven arrows pierce the sky. "They can waste their arrows, men; we wait for them to meet us; we will take cover and let them waste their ammo; we will then unleash hell!" shouted Ironfist.

The battle had begun, and all across Skell, the factions prepared for a war that would decide the fate of the island—once and for all.

Chapter Fifteen

Marcella adjusted the draw length on her new toy, turning the screw in her compound bow's cam. As the rest of the human army offloaded their gear, allowing crates and fabric-bound bundles to settle in the beach's sandy dunes, her father watched the process with more than a passing interest.

Cael asked, "How many of these things do we have?"

Without looking up, Marcella replied, "Fifty."

The King nodded slowly. He murmured, "I suppose that's fine. If one of these 'compound bowmen' falls, someone else can recover the weapon and use it."

"Not really, father. They require intense training to use properly, and the draw length and pull strength are tailored to the owner."

Cael snorted and scowled. "And they're delicate as well?"

"Oh, yes. Very."

He threw his hands up and started to stomp his way up the beach. "You and your love for technology. This is supposed to turn the tide?"

Marcella glanced up, wounded by her father's tone. Then, her keen eyes found a speck of black in the sky above, circling lazily above the beach. Her right hand flicked back over her shoulder to grab an arrow from her quiver. She took a breath. Aimed. And released.

As the human King mumbled and headed towards the main landing site, a couple of soldiers shouted out warnings. He paused just in time to avoid the bird's corpse as it plummeted out of the sky and landed at his booted feet in a bloody heap.

Half startled, Cael just stared at the dead raven, impaled by one of his daughter's steel arrows. She walked up the beach to rejoin him just as he stooped to pluck the leather band off of the messenger bird's leg and unfurl the message. Sadly, it was in the elven tongue.

A smaller hand covered his wrist. Marcella murmured, "If they can't communicate, they can't coordinate. We will just destroy it, your Highness."

He nodded slowly and felt her fingers slip away as his daughter turned so that she could rendezvous with her unit.

"Marcella."

"Father?"

"Your mother would be proud."

He heard her breath hitch and catch in her chest. Then, her footsteps crunched in the sand as she walked away.

He murmured to himself, "Good girl. Duty first. There's work to be done."

Unbeknownst to the Cael, a second invasion force had landed on the other side of the tropical fjord. The tall cliffs that flanked the twin inlets obscured the humans' vision of the dwarves and vice versa. Neither army was particularly quiet, but the wind funnelling north through the twisting seaside canyons didn't carry the din of disembarking or preparation east to west.

So Tholgar had no idea that his people weren't alone. Nor did Baldric, who was in the hastily assembled royal tent, busily strapping his King into his armour. The coastal wind nearly collapsed the tanned leather structure a couple of times, but it managed to hold firm.

"Did you remember to talcum your thighs, old man?"

Tholgar snorted and made as if to draw his sword. "Did you remember I could end your life with an order?"

Baldric smirked and tightened up the final strap. He was one of the only soldiers who could get away with talking to his King that way; he'd been at his monarch's side for his entire life. He rumbled, "Seriously, though. It could be a long hike. Will you be riding at all?"

Tholgar considered. Then he nodded and said, "On and off. It's important that the troops see their King marching side by side with them, at least when we set off."

"Aye, Your Highness. I'll see you out there."

"Aye. Don't die, Baldric."

"Don't die, old man."

Tholgar closed his eyes for a moment. He centred himself, willing his thundering heartbeat to slow.

Moments later, the dwarven King threw the tent's flaps open and strode out. The troops cheered, and the war elephants trumpeted.

He addressed his people, "First, we get onto those cliffs, then we march until we find the capital!"

The sound of the wind and the waves was obliterated by the boisterous cheer that followed.

The Elves had been preparing for this moment for days, waiting silently on the eastern cliffs overlooking the fjord. A thousand archers stood ready, their bows poised to rain death upon any who dared invade their lands. Each elf moved with purpose, their lithe bodies hidden within the natural contours of the rocky landscape, blending seamlessly with the earth and trees. They had honed their skills for centuries, and now, their arrows were nocked, aimed, and drawn, just waiting for the signal to release.

Alongside the archers, four hundred foot soldiers held their ground, their swords sheathed, shields glinting faintly in the sun that peeked through the cloud cover. The cliffside was a fortress, a natural barricade that provided the Elves with a strategic advantage. Below them, they could see both the two camps of the human and dwarven armies assembling on the beach, unaware of the danger lurking above.

The Elves had the high ground, and they were patient. Every elf warrior knew that once the enemy began their march north through the dense jungle, they'd be perfectly within range of their deadly barrage. From their vantage point, they could see the humans unloading their supplies and organising their troops—blissfully unaware of the impending strike.

General Laerion Stood on the edge of the cliff, watching deviously.

"Men, it's time!" he screamed." Formation 44 at the double. MOVE, MOVE, MOVE."

The elven archers quickly scrambled into formation.

A line of 100 men long formed. First, a shield wall was made, angled down towards the beach, the shields practically hanging off the cliff whilst the men holding them crouched uncomfortably so they could keep their arms out fully stretched and sturdy without being in the way of the three lines of bowmen stood behind.

The human army crept north and started to give way to marshy moss as the jungle dominated their collective vision. They were less than fifty metres from the rubbery canopy of leaves when the first volley hit. After every round of fire, there was a few seconds of calm before the next barrage of arrows filled the sky.

Arrows rained down from the eastern cliffside, the elves using the fjord's natural features to their full advantage. Dozens of soldiers screamed as the bodkin points pierced their chainmail and leather. Whilst only a fraction of these hits were fatal, the elves knew that caring for a wounded soldier was far more labour than caring for a dead one.

Cael barked, "Shield wall! Up and continue."

The infantry scrambled to obey and managed to assemble a reasonable barrier before the next volley of arrows hit. Medics scrambled to drag the wounded to safety and to end the suffering of those who were too far gone to save.

But the elves hadn't counted on Marcella. Her four dozen archers, armed with the most advanced bows on the planet, crowded behind three of the supply wagons and waited for her orders.

As soon as the second volley of elven arrows began to fall, she said, "Two volleys of counterfire, then scramble. Find any cover you can; rocks, logs, or make it to the jungle's edge. Remember your training."

The distinct twang of fifty compound bows firing at once was new to elven ears. But as the projectiles began to break through the shield wall and find the chests, arms, and eye sockets of their most elite marksmen, it became clear that Death would remain unbiased that day.

On the other side of the cliff face, The dwarves were similarly pinned down. They had suffered fewer casualties than the humans, thanks to their higher quality mail. But they stood no chance of making a run for the jungle's edge, their short legs not exactly equipped for a sprint of that nature.

One of the scouts reported that there was a pathway that circled up to the back of the plateau, but it started thirty metres past the lip of the jungle's edge. Again, it wasn't much of an option.

Baldric gritted his teeth as another arrow shattered off of his raised shield. It was one of half a dozen protecting King Tholgar Ironfist from an untimely death.

The King bellowed, "Get word back to the ships: Roll out the deck cannons under a second shield wall! We'll shatter the side of that cliff."

The messenger didn't look very confident in her monarch's plan. Nevertheless, she nodded and sprinted back down the beach, barely dodging an arrow on the way back to the closest warship. One of the war elephants had been taken out by a lucky shot to the eye... unfortunate, but it did provide the messenger with some much-needed cover on her journey.

Baldric asked, "Do we want to move, Your Highness?"

Tholgar's reply was surprisingly calm. "No. The last volley was weaker than the first."

"What...how do you know?"

"I told you that you need to open your damned ears in battle, Baldric. The impacts. Something is picking off those archers."

The soldier's mind raced. He cursed roundly as another arrow hit, and the shattered wood splintered and embedded in his right cheek. After a moment, he asked, "Perhaps we are not the only ones on this beach?"

"I'm not sure. But if they give us an opening, we're damned well going to find out."

Marcella wedged herself under a driftwood log and clutched her scalp, willing the blood to stop or at least to slow as she fumbled with the cotton underlining of her leather armour. Finally, she managed to rip a long strip free. Quickly, she bandaged up the gash that a broadhead arrow had carved across her left temple.

After clearing the blood from her eyes, she risked a peek over the top of the log and saw that her compound bow brigade had created enough chaos for her father to act. A hundred sappers, wearing mostly hide and leather, scrambled up the treacherous side path that wound up to the rear of the plateau that the elves were using as a base of operations. The more heavily armoured sword brigade was making slower progress, but at least they weren't being cut down en masse.

As she tied off the makeshift bandage, an arrow buried itself in the log, no less than 8 centimetres from her jugular vein. She wiped her crimson-stained hand in the sand and then against the side of the log before reaching back for her next arrow. It seemed that the enemy archers still had it out for her.

That was fine. She needed a bit more target practice.

Tholgar listened to the rhythm of arrows hitting shields, as calm as a maiden listening to fat raindrops hitting the roof of her cottage. After a particularly weak array of impacts, he made the call.

"Get a move on! King's guard, to the jungle path. Double time!"

Baldric opened his mouth to protest. There was no way that he should be allowing the King to personally charge up to confront those archers. But one look in his monarch's eyes was all it took to silence those protests forever.

The mad, shuffling charge across the sand wasn't accompanied by complaints or cries of fear. In typical dwarven fashion, the madness of battle was met with laughter.

The ground trembled beneath the thunderous weight of the war elephants as they charged through the opening of the jungle terrain at the foot of the cliffs. These towering beasts, draped in thick golden armour, were causing chaos for the elves.

Each elephant was a walking fortress, with massive crossbows mounted on their backs, manned by expert dwarven marksmen. The armour plating clanged with each heavy step, adding to the deafening roar of their advance as they flattened trees and bushes, leaving a path of destruction in their wake.

With their enormous crossbows drawn, the dwarven soldiers took careful aim at the elven shield wall. The bolts they fired were no ordinary arrows—they were massive, spear-like projectiles, each one capable of cutting through multiple bodies.

As the first volley was released, the air seemed to hiss with the speed of the enormous bolts. The result was brutal. The projectiles sliced through the elven ranks, punching through shields, armour, and bodies, felling three or four warriors at a time in a single, unrelenting strike. Guts and blood exploded on impact, and screams of terror came from the elven swordsmen who were still spectators at this point.

The elephants pressed forward, unyielding, their golden armour reflecting the flickers of sunlight that broke through the shattered forest canopy. The dwarves atop them reloaded their crossbows with ruthless efficiency, each shot aimed to break the elven defences further, widening the breach for the inevitable full-on assault. Trees snapped and groaned under the relentless advance, and the ground was soon littered with the splintered remains of both the forest and the fallen.

“Swordsmen of Heavans keep, take the knees of those elephants, take them down,” screamed the Elven General Laerion in desperation; he couldn’t bear it anymore.

The elven swordsmen, desperate and determined, surged forward as General Laerion’s command echoed through the chaos of battle.

The elven swordsmen charged down the cliffs, blades drawn, but were quickly overwhelmed. Arrows rained down, piercing throats and felling them like leaves in the wind. Those who survived the volley faced the rampaging war elephants, their trunks sweeping through the ranks, crushing ribcages, and hurling men into the air like ragdolls. The few who reached the beasts struck desperately at the golden armour, but their attacks were futile. One elf managed to drive his sword into an elephant's toe, only to be crushed instantly beneath its massive foot, flattened like a pancake; his life snuffed out in a heartbeat.

In their attempts to disable the elephants, many of the elven swordsmen found themselves trampled beneath the beasts' massive feet. Their lithe, agile forms were no match for the overwhelming weight and power of the elephants, and the forest floor quickly became a graveyard of crushed bodies, the blood of hundreds flowing like wine. The elephants pressed forward, heedless of the soldiers beneath them, their golden armour gleaming even as blood splattered across it. Trees snapped like brittle bones, and the once-proud elven warriors were reduced to mere obstacles in the path of destruction.

The elves fought bravely; the sight of their comrades being impaled or crushed was demoralising. However, each moment of distraction by the swordsmen, each desperate attempt to bring the giants down, only gave the elven archers above more time to continue their assault from the cliffs. Arrows rained down on the dwarves and humans, but the chaos on the ground made the elves' aim increasingly less effective.

The two groups made it up the treacherous rear path to the top of the cliffs at the same time. Wide-eyed, the brave men of Blackhaven were suddenly face-to-face with the most well-armed and armoured little people that they had ever seen. Clubs, short swords, and nets would do next to nothing against such a force.

Tholgar eyed the humans. He'd seen them before on the open sea, mostly at a distance from the shores of Hammerdeep. They tended not to mess with the dwarves. Today, he had to trust that such wise decision-making would continue to hold true.

The dwarven King barked, "Form up, make a wedge! Get the tall ones up to the archers, and we end this."

Disciplined to a fault, the dwarves immediately turned to the left and got into position. They freely offered the humans their flank.

After a moment of hesitation, the sapper leader shouted, "Crouch low until our new friends have broken their lines. Then do what we do best, boys."

For the first time in over two centuries, a mixed dwarven and human force charged into battle against a common foe.

Cael watched in disbelief as screaming elves started to bounce down the side of the sheer cliff face. Some of them had gaping axe wounds; others were hopelessly entangled in nets. A few couldn't scream because they already had their heads caved in. But by the time the bodies rolled to a stop in the sands below, all of them were most certainly dead.

Marcella slowly made her way over to her father's side. He tore his gaze from the virtual waterfall of corpses long enough to wince at her head wound. He reached up to examine it but had his hand slapped away by the irritated princess.

He murmured, "Are you okay?."

She peered up at the slaughter in progress. "They are not from Blackhaven. Who are they?"

"Allies, my dear. I think, at this point, we have to call them our allies."

Chapter Sixteen

The elven war council sat at the gold-inlaid oak table in a special war room behind the royal throne. It was reserved for official state emergencies. As was tradition, it was only used for serious matters, mostly war.

The older elves silently read the reports of the coastal battle that saw two of the Kingdom's rivals band together. King Zelder, having already reviewed the disastrous events of the past week, paces behind his chair which sat at the end of the table.

Elandril, the council's senior diplomat, murmured. "Dear sweet mercy."

Zeldar snapped, "Which part did you read, my esteemed advisor?"

"Your Majesty. I—"

"Was it the fact that around 90% of our eastern battalion was cut down?" the King asked.

Laerion, the commander of the elven army, sighed and set down his report. "Your Majesty."

Zeldar ignored the older elf's chiding tone, snapping at the other man, "Or maybe, my Lord Commander, it was the fact that enemy losses were only estimated at 15%? Or that they kept every single one of their ships? You only managed to kill one Dwarven elephant?"

Laerion simply bent his head and went back to reading the details of the slaughter.

Elandril, the council's senior diplomat, set down his stack of papers with shaking hands. He swallowed hard before suggesting, "Perhaps we should see if there's still a deal on the table with one of the other factions?"

That suggestion had the King's voice dripping with sarcasm. "Who would you suggest we turn to, Elandril? The wolves who we slaughtered mercilessly on the field of battle? Or the orks, who have been raping and pillaging their way through the southern reaches and are less than a day from our very doorstep?"

Before the monarch could wither the diplomat any further, Nioma, the council's magical advisor, spoke. "Perhaps His Majesty would consider joining us down below, where we're working on adapting your dear lost sister's magic to run off of the arcane power of the magic still inside the bunker?"

King Zelder actually considered that, pausing in his back-and-forth prowling. Then he shook his head angrily. "That was her legacy, not mine. Anyway, how is that even an option? We have no idea how to harness it, and we have no idea why it's still there! I would just be a distraction down there. Whatever you're working on to bolster our defences, get it done, but forget about Elaena! Raid the treasury, call in every esoteric expert. Whatever you need!"

Nioma rose, tucking the battle report under her left arm before bowing. "It will be done, my King."

"Good. Laerion. The orks. What do we do about the damned orks?"

The commander stood slowly. He took a deep breath before answering, "Most of the fire giants are still north, though we do have some of them close to the capital. The entirety of the National Defense Force and the King's Guard are available. We've always said that defence of this city, of your throne, was paramount."

These words seemed to mollify Zelder somewhat. He huffed out a frustrated sigh but admitted, "If we can stop that insane horde of murderers in their tracks, the main threat will have been crushed. The humans and dwarves are far more... or I should say, they're far less..."

He trailed off.

Elandril offered, "Demonic?"

“I suppose. Laerion, assemble the troops before this evening’s meal. I’ll address them personally. And quietly. There are enough rumours circulating amongst the citizenry; no need to add to that mess.”

“Yes, my King. It shall be done.”

King Zelder looked at each of his advisors in order to see if they had anything else to say. With no further advice coming, the King of the elves strode out of his throne room. The last thing that the advisors heard before the discrete side door slammed was their monarch’s frustrated scream.

Gron Ironfang looked over the remains of his army. He had less than three-quarters of his original force of 10,000. The loss of troops had very little to do with the resistance they’d faced on the southern coast... All told he lost less than 400 soldiers on the campaign.

No, his forces had been depleted by opportunity. Many of the minor clans that had followed his banner to the new world splintered off once the first elven communities had been captured or raised. That was their right, of course; every clan’s leader could end their campaign as they saw fit. Gron could have challenged and slaughtered those leaders to bring their soldiers under the Redaxe Clan’s banner.

But the thought of thousands of orcs scattered across the southern side of the continent, looting and breeding their way through every elven house they found, brought a fanged smile to Gron's face. This was how it was meant to be.

Besides, he still had the three largest ork clans on his side. Six thousand eight hundred braves should be more than enough to finish their campaign and bring these skinny debutants to heel.

Raggok glanced up and to the left and saw his leader grinning like a madman. The assembled troops, some still in the process of breaking camp, shifted restlessly as they awaited their grinning leader's command.

He leaned over and whispered, "Sir? The men."

Gron blinked, caught deep in his thoughts. He slapped his loyal guard on the back of the head, then straightened his shoulders to address the troops.

"Mount Morvem hides Heavens Keep; this is where the King of the Rats is holed up with his advisors. It is the source of the Elven command. We. Must. Reach. It!"

Gron thrust his axe in the air. The resulting howl was near-deafening. Surely, the elves heard it in their prissy little palace.

He couldn't help but grin again. It would be a battle for the ages.

At nightfall, the orcs made camp, setting up fires and sharpening weapons, eager for the next day's bloodshed. As the sun rose, Gron Ironfang rallied his army, and they marched towards the elven capital. By midday, they reached the fields of Haleinde, where elven forces waited.

As the elves stood atop the hill overlooking the fields of Haleinde, their hearts sank at the sight before them. A massive sea of orcs stretched far across the horizon, their ranks seemingly endless. The air was thick with the pounding of war drums and the guttural cries of the orcish horde. The ground trembled beneath the weight of thousands of war boars, and in the distance, the eerie glow of dragonites' flames flickered.

General Laerion's eyes shifted uneasily to King Zelder, who sat tall upon his royal war horse, a magnificent creature bred for both speed and grace. The horse's coat was pure white, gleaming even in the dim light, and its flowing mane matched, cascading like silver threads in the wind. The animal wore lightweight elven armour crafted from diamond-cut plates that shimmered faintly, protecting without hindering its movement. Its hooves, polished and strong, pawed at the ground, sensing the tension in the air.

Laerion met the King's gaze, his voice low with concern. "Your Grace, the Orks—there are too many. Even with our archers, it will be difficult to hold them. Many of our best men died on the cliffs of Selthore Shores."

King Zelder's face was calm, his eyes hard as flint as he surveyed the approaching horde. "Form a shield wall starting there," the King said as he pointed to a flat, vast opening around 50 meters from his men. "We start with the archers; we fire until we have no arrows left," he commanded, his voice steady but firm. "Let them come. We will not waste our swordsmen until we have thinned their numbers."

Laerion gave a curt nod, though the unease in his chest remained. The King, atop his brilliant war horse, seemed unfazed, but the general knew the weight of their situation. "As you wish, my King," Laerion replied, his hand resting on the hilt of his sword as he turned to give the order.

The King's white steed snorted, its muscles rippling under the delicate armour as if eager to charge, but it stood still, awaiting its master's next move. The archers prepared behind them, bows drawn, ready to obey.

Gron Ironfang stood tall before his assembled army, his massive green form silhouetted against the rising sun. His blood-red axe glinted in the morning light, and the guttural murmur of Orkish braves quieted as they awaited their warlord's words. Gron's yellow eyes burned with fierce pride, scanning the thousands of Orcs ready for battle, their warpaint vivid against their scarred skin.

He raised his axe high, and a primal silence fell over the horde.

With a voice that rumbled like thunder, he began:

“Brothers. Hear me now!”

The Orks responded with a low growl of anticipation, their fists clenching around axes, swords, and spears.

“These lands… **they are ours**! These weak, pointy-eared wretches, these elves who cower in their towers—**they think they can stop us!**” His voice grew louder, more venomous. “They believe their walls, their arrows, and their precious magic can keep us from taking what belongs to us!”

The horde roared in agreement, a sea of shifting bodies and tensing muscles, preparing for the slaughter to come.

“But I see what they cannot! **I see victory!** I see your axes cutting through their necks! I see your blades drinking deep from their noble throats!”

He paused, lowering his voice just enough to let the tension build. His eyes scanned the crowd, locking onto the eager warriors at the front.

“I see their cities burning. Their lands were covered in the banners of **OUR CLANS**! I see the skulls of their kings and generals at our feet!”

Another roar erupted from the horde, louder this time, filled with the bloodlust they were known for.

“We have taken their coasts and mountains to the south; we have slain Thrarxis, and today, we finish what we started! Today, we claim their capital, and the last of their kind will fall to the might of the Orkish Men of Gruk'Thor.”

The orcs were now in a frenzy of battle cries, shaking their weapons and pounding their shields.

“So charge, my warriors! Let the earth tremble beneath our feet! Let their blood run like rivers! And when the sun sets, we will feast on their bones and stand victorious atop their shattered kingdom!”

With a final, deafening roar, Gron thrust his axe towards the sky, signalling the charge, and growled at the top of his lungs, “For our ancestors!”

The first line of orcs surged forward across the open fields, a wild, ragtag group of low-skilled swordsmen. Their armour was crude—leather straps, rusted mail, and scavenged pieces of iron—and their weapons were a chaotic mix of axes, swords, and jagged, curved blades. Shields of mismatched wood and bone rattled as they sprinted, their guttural battle cries tearing through the morning air.

The orcs thundered ahead, their heavy footfalls kicking up dirt and dust in their wake. The grass beneath their boots flattened under the weight of their charge, and the distance between them and the elven army closed rapidly.

From the elven lines, the sound of horns echoed, sharp and clear, and the first volley of arrows was loosed. The sky darkened momentarily as thousands of finely crafted elven arrows sailed through the air, their points glinting in the sun.

A terrible rain of death fell upon the charging orcs. Arrows pierced their ranks, punching through shields and flesh alike. Screams of pain mixed with the pounding of feet as the front ranks staggered. Some fell instantly, arrows lodged deep in their necks or chests, blood spurting across the battlefield. Others, driven by rage, pulled arrows from their limbs and kept running, their eyes wild with fury. The ground became slick with the blood of their fallen, but still, they pressed forward, unstoppable.

Closer now, the orcs smashed into the elven shield wall. The sound of iron clashing against elven steel echoed across the field. The orcs swung their weapons wildly, crashing into the elven defenders with raw, brute strength. Their curved swords struck against the polished elven shields and axes splintered wood, but the elves held firm, disciplined, their phalanx barely budging.

The fight had begun in earnest. Orcs hacked and slashed, their uncoordinated attacks met by the precision of the elven soldiers. Behind the shield wall, elven spears darted forward, skewering orcs through gaps in their defence. The battlefield rang with the sounds of battle—swords clanging, shields splintering, and the guttural roars of the orc animalistic horde locked in deadly combat with the poised and methodical elven forces.

Gron quickly recognised that his first wave of lowly skilled men had done their job. They had made it to the enemy; now it was time for the main event.

"Giant War boars form a line; Chaplin, get your Dragonites ready," Gron Shouted.

The Chaplin of Fire started chanting to himself in ancient Orkish with eyes rolled back. The Dragonites were let out of their cages, hundreds at a time, before surrounding the Chaplin.

"Men, you know what to do, no survivors, charge!" Gron Demanded.

A thousand giant war boars thundered across the open plains, their massive bodies glistening in the sunlight. Each beast was a formidable sight, armoured in thick, iron plating that gleamed with a menacing sheen. The sound of their hooves pounding the earth was like distant thunder, a deep rumble that sent vibrations through the ground.

The elven archers loosed a flurry of arrows, the projectiles raining down upon the charging horde. But the war boars surged forward, seemingly unfazed by the onslaught. The arrows bounced harmlessly off their thick armour or clattered to the ground, defeated before they could even pierce the hide of these titanic creatures. A few errant shots found their mark, embedding into the flesh of the beasts, but their sheer muscle and brute strength carried them onward, undeterred.

Above the chaos, Dragonites soared through the sky, their miniature wings beating rapidly. Their scales glimmered with hues of crimson and gold as they banked and circled, surveying the ground below with keen, predatory eyes. Occasionally, they would let out an unpleasant squeal, a sound that reverberated through the air and sent shivers down the spines of those who dared to look up. They were waiting for the right time to dive down and join the fray. Their presence heightened the tension in the air.

Gron Ironfang, surveying the scene, noted his diminished forces—just over 6,000 of the original 10,000 remained. But his confidence never wavered. The battle was far from over, and with the might of the orc clans still under his command, he knew they could crush the elven resistance once and for all.

The fall of the elven capital was not a sudden event but a slow, agonising descent into ruin. As the orcish horde drew closer, King Zelder had to save as many of his people as possible. The orc invasion had already decimated the southern regions of the capital, burning small farms and murdering innocent people on their way up.

The city's destruction had already started as giant boulders catapulted towards the walls, leaving a trail of destruction deep within the streets, the boulders flattening houses like bowling balls do pins. Supplies had started weeks ago as the ork raids cut off trade routes to the south.

King Zelder acted swiftly; he issued the royal decree for a mass evacuation, sacrificing a hundred men from his army to escort the people to safety. Thousands of families were ordered to leave immediately. Soldiers, dressed in gleaming elven armour, pointed the terrified citizens towards the northern gates of the city, urging citizens to pack only what they could carry. The streets of the capital, once bustling with trade and life, became clogged with families hastily fleeing whilst deafening screams filled the broken streets. Carts filled with personal belongings creaked along the cobblestone roads, crying children clutched their parents' hands, and younger relatives assisted the elderly, their faces lined with sorrow and fear.

Zelder had chosen the towns of Montoise and Seacry as the primary evacuation points. These northern settlements had been untouched by the devastation wrought by the snow people. According to reports, both towns were still secure, their defences bolstered, and their people were ready to receive the evacuees. It was a calculated risk, but the King hoped that sending his people to these relatively safe havens would preserve their way of life, at least for a little while longer.

As the evacuation proceeded, the city itself slowly crumbled. With every passing minute, more homes were abandoned. Markets that once thrived with exotic goods from across the realm stood empty or destroyed, their stalls deserted or gone. The grand libraries of the city, filled with ancient elven lore and centuries of knowledge, were locked and sealed, their secrets left behind in the rush to escape.

Murder, and fall back. Murder, and fall back. The elven archers made the long retreat through the city and started to climb to the Royal Palace. They picked off hundreds of brave Orkish warriors before finding themselves pinned up against the palace walls.

As the drawbridge was being lowered, a guttural voice began to chant from just around the final bend in the King's Highway. The Chaplin of Fire began his prayer, and thousands of little sky devils screeched over with the chant.

The first elven scream happened when one of the faster Dragites tore off half of the man's face. This set off a panic among the archers, who had their choice between the spiked pit in front of them or the mass of tiny fire-breathing creatures darkening the eastern sky.

The creatures swarmed the lightly armoured elves, breathing gouts of chemical flame into their eyes, melting their shrinking faces as others feasted on that warm, sweet, elven flesh. Diving off the side of the dry moat was no mercy for the elves, as their spike-impaled, dying bodies were feasted upon by hungry dragite mothers looking to feed their brood.

By the time the drawbridge was three-quarters of the way down, there were no archers left to save. Progress was arrested, the chains groaning as the elven guards tried to pull the massive oak and iron bridge back up.

But the Orkish berserkers had caught up at that point. Using the burning and bleeding archer corpses as a vaulting point, a dozen madmen leapt and caught the lip of the drawbridge. Half a dozen more failed and fell into the spike pit below, singing praises to the clan as they plummeted to their death. The ones who made it chopped away the wood surrounding the chains' support structure. The drawbridge cracked at the corners and fell into place with a shuddering thud.

The oOrkishhorde charged across the bridge and into the courtyard, beheading the small team of gate operators without a thought. The palace was in sight now.

Suddenly, in the distance arrived the fire giants. Kragor and half a dozen of his kin stood at the front of the elven King's Guard. The well-armoured, highly disciplined troops stood behind the giants, platinum-tipped pikes at the ready. Behind them, more archers, of course, the elves' favourite clean-up squad.

The dragites were first in, but their breath of fire did nothing to the red-skinned giants. Their bites simply anchored them in place. The Chaplin of Fire cried out in grief as the fire giants summoned the power of the lava to immolate the surface of their skin. The air turned brown as the dragite boiled within their flesh, falling to the flagstones and disintegrating, nothing but crisp carbon at that point. The few tiny creatures that remained scattered, their survival instincts kicking in. They would go to nest in the south foothills to feed the next generation and rebuild their numbers.

Next were the berserkers. The ones that weren't cut down by arrows were crushed by the giants' stomping feet. Lava and flame-seared their flesh as they were crushed flat, cooking them against the flagstones like overdone bacon.

Gron Ironfang watched as the bulk of his army started to charge across the fallen drawbridge. He scowled. Such a narrow entryway meant that he couldn't use the full might of his forces. After the first few hundred soldiers thundered past, Gron started to shoulder his way inside.

A meaty hand fell on his arm. Raggok. His eyes were wide, and he was shaking his head. "Let them work, sire."

Gron snarled at his loyal guard, easily brushing off the restraining hand. Without a word, he slipped into the flow of green bodies surging towards the front line.

Raggok cursed roundly. He dove into the flow of orks, doing his best to keep up with his King.

As hundreds of orks flooded into the courtyard in an attempt to surround the giants, Wout stuck to the shadows. As much as he would have loved to get his axe dirty, he had a special quest. The elven peasants had bragged about the prowess of the fire giant King as they were being raided by the tribes on their long journey north towards Ardenviel. So Wout had prepared a few special toys to even the odds. He crouched behind one of the marble statues of the elves' accursed magical princess. Carefully, he filled three threaded glass vials with water and the white dust he'd extracted by drying out starfish. As the mixture hissed and bubbled, he quickly screwed the vials into three iron spears created just for this moment.

The Orkish army crashed against the King's Guard like a tidal wave against a sheer cliff face. Some of the fire giants, wary about getting flanked, turned to witness the resulting carnage. Pike impaled the frontline of the orks and even pierced into some of the next ranks but swiftly became useless against the press of bodies. Orcish axes cleaved the fine helmets of many elves before they managed to transition to their standard-issue longswords.

Kragor was just about to call for order in his ranks when he doubled over and howled in pain as the first vial-tipped spear shattered against his right hip. The chemical ice spread from the point of impact of Wout's spear, turning the lava on the fire giant King's hip to a black, glassy obsidian. The massive creature nearly kept his balance, but the second spear struck him in the left knee. In utter agony, the fire giant leader fell. It was little consolation that he crushed half a dozen orks on the way down. The flash of axes working in tandem quickly separated Kragor's head from his body, ending a legacy of tireless service.

The remaining fire giants froze in place for a moment, pausing their rampage of destruction through the Orkish ranks. They began glowing a bright cherry red, their link with the mountain's magic slipping out of their grasp as grief and rage took control. Waves of unbearable heat began to flood the courtyard.

Gron, approaching the front line, watched with unblinking eyes as the fire giant closest to him started to swell. Cracks appeared in the massive creature's skin, and hissing magma started to escape under the pressure.

The ork King turned to see Raggok, who had just caught up with him. He saw the acceptance of death in the eyes of his second in command…of his friend.

Gron smirked. Then he shoved Raggok with all his might. The shocked warrior traversed a good fifth of the courtyard before tumbling to a stop next to Wout. Always quick-witted, the young soldier yanked Raggok behind the massive statue of Elaena just as the disaster unfolded.

A half dozen fire giants' mouths exploded with fire before exhaling it out towards the orks. Those not close enough to be killed by the river of fire were inundated with waves of bubbling lava. It cooled quickly in the air, becoming sheets of jagged obsidian. But not before the damage was done.

After the waves of heat died down, Wout peeked out from behind his improvised cover. Behind him, well over four-fifths of the Orkish army was either ash and bones or buried in a river of glassy black stone. To the west, the final battle between the King's Guard and the orks was immortalised in volcanic stone, their half-melted figures locked in battle forever. The back entryway to the castle was sealed in several tons of still-cooling obsidian.

Concussed, Raggok staggered out to join Wout. After a confused moment, he picked up a fallen axe and started trudging away from the fight.

Raggok grabbed his shoulder. "It's over! We need to save what's left of us."

The young Wout turned to regard him. More softly, the young warrior said, "It's over. We'd have to go all the way around to do a frontal assault, and they'll be waiting. All of them will be ready."

Wout grunted. He half lowered his axe as he looked to the spot where Gron had last stood. There was nothing but ash.

“You need to lead our people now.”

“Lead ‘em where?” said Raggok.

“We still hold the South,” Wout replied.

Raggok took a deep breath. Outside the courtyard and across the now-obsidian bridge, the survivors of his clan and many others fled. He straightened up, brushed himself off, and moved to join them. But not before saying, “I need a right-hand man.”

Wout snorted and began to follow. “I’m not that stupid.”

“Fine. I’ll ask you again after your third bottle of mead. For the moment, help me get our people out of this hellscape.”

The younger orc nodded. They set off down the mountain pass and back towards the fertile eastern plains, where their brothers and sisters awaited their return.

As the mixed unit of dwarves and humans emerged from the jungle, Cael was finally able to get a clear view of the castle on the mountain. A horrific scene unfolded before them.

The city walls, once a formidable barrier, lay in crumbled heaps, their stones scattered across the ground like fallen giants.

Houses that had once stood proudly, filled with life and laughter, were now reduced to charred skeletons, their remnants smouldering in the aftermath of the conflict. The acrid scent of smoke hung heavy in the air, mingling with the metallic tang of blood, creating an oppressive atmosphere that spoke of the violence that had unfolded.

As they advanced, the sight of thousands of bodies littering the fields surrounding the city walls sent a chill down their spines. Elven warriors, their faces frozen in expressions of defiance and fear, lay amidst the rubble whilstOrkishh brutes, clad in mismatched armour, lay torched and butchered by arrows.

The ground was a gruesome tapestry of despair: blood-soaked earth and discarded weapons formed a stark contrast against the backdrop of smouldering ruins. Deep imprints marked the soil where giant war boars had charged, leaving behind evidence of their brutal rampage.

As the humans and dwarves exchanged worried glances, the full scale of the devastation became undeniable.

King Cael murmured, “What a sight.”

Tholgar replied quietly, “Aye, what a sight indeed. It seems our Orkish friends have had it out with the Elves. Not sure who won, though.” He laughed.

Marcella shouldered her bow and drew even with her father. She seemed unbothered by the sight and murmured, “How did we not hear this? There must have been thousands of them fighting.”

Cael slowly shook his head. Once the troops were clear of the treeline, he ordered, “Assemble the cannons in the valley below the mountain path!”

Tholgar made his way over to the human. He peered up at the castle. “I expected more resistance than this.”

The human King said, “As did I. I think we are too late.”

Baldric placed his weapon back on his hip along with his King. He shook his head and pointed up to the castle far above. “They’re still flying the elven flag and colours.”

The three others stared at him. It was his King who had to ask, “Did you steal an eagle’s eyes when I wasn’t looking?”

“No, no. I stole the spyglass from one of our ship captains. Commandeered, really.”

The four turned and stared up at the object of their conquest. After a beat, Tholgar shouted, “Assemble the siege engines behind the human cannon line. I want firing solutions for the castle on the trebuchets and ballista firing solutions for the two main bends in the road leading up to that accursed place.”

As the dwarven engineers set to work and the support caravans began to set up camp, the two Kings made plans for a short, brutal siege for the next few days whilst they scouted out the elven or Orkish army. Whoever it was who survived.

Days passed in tense silence as the siege surrounding Ardenviel dragged on, the once-vibrant city now shrouded in an eerie stillness. The humans and dwarves camped at the outskirts, with no signs of life emerging from the ruins; uncertainty began to seep into their ranks.

The human king, his brow scowling with concern, gathered his closest advisors around a makeshift campfire. The flickering flames illuminated their weary faces, revealing deep lines etched from worry and fatigue. "We cannot linger here indefinitely," he declared, his voice low but resolute. "The longer we wait, the more we risk losing everything. We need food, and we need to know what has become of the elves."

Beside him stood the dwarven leader, his armoured frame imposing even in the flickering light. Tholgar Ironfist surveyed the remnants of the city through narrowed eyes, his expression grim. "Aye, I agree," he replied. "But we cannot send a large force into the city. The orks or elves may still be lurking within those ruins, and our numbers are already too few; a lot of men are hungry and weak."

After a brief silence, the king nodded. "Then we will send a small band—a hundred brave souls, skilled and swift. They can scout the city, gather information, and report back. If it is clear, we can move our forces in and reclaim what's ours."

With a determined glint in his eye, Tholgar added, "Let us choose the best among us. Those who are not afraid to face whatever horrors may await within those walls."

Thus, a contingent of one hundred men was assembled, each soldier steeling himself for the unknown. They readied their weapons, their hearts heavy with a mix of dread and hope, knowing they might be venturing into a trap or a grave. As the sun dipped below the horizon, casting long shadows across the great stone walls of Ardenviel, the small band set forth towards the city, their footsteps careful around the thousands of dead, stinking bodies lying in puddles of blood and mud.

"Halt," shouted King Cael, his fist raised clenched above his head. "Tholgar, can you feel it?"

Tholgar stood in a stance as though he was about to fight for his life; his eyes scanned the ruins ahead like an eagle looking for prey as it patrolled the skies. "Shh," Tholgar hushed his men.

Tension rapidly grew amongst the mixed crop of braves.

Out of nowhere, an arrow pierced through the skull of a human, entering the eye before leaving again quickly to the rear. And as that man fell to the ground, the elves revealed themselves.

The elves, far fewer in number than the advancing forces of opposition, could not meet them in open combat. Instead, they used what was left of the city to their advantage. They had hidden expertly among the ruins, turning the broken landscape into an invisible line of defence. Archers crouched silently on the rooftops of half-collapsed houses. They hid behind windows on the upper levels of any remaining houses whilst occasionally taking a small peak, their sleek, silver arrows nocked and ready to fire. Elven Swordsmen, their lithe forms blending with the shadows, lay in wait inside the hollowed-out ruins, prepared to ambush anyone walking the blood-stained cobbled streets. It was a strategy born of necessity.

“Arrows!” dwarven swordmen shouted, raising a shield just in time to deflect another deadly projectile. Chaos erupted as the elves unleashed their final defence, trying to repel the invaders with the little strength they had left.

“Shield wall! Archers, pick them off!” Cael commanded, his voice cutting through the chaos. The men sprang into action, swiftly forming an impenetrable testudo-style formation, their shields interlocking to create a solid barrier that sealed off the street. Archers took position behind the shield-bearers, releasing volleys between the gaps. As they reloaded, the front rows raised their shields high, forming a protective canopy, effectively shielding the entire unit from the elven arrows raining down from the rooftops above.

A few tense minutes passed, and one by one, the elven archers fell. The opposing arrows found their marks, cutting down the hidden enemies perched on rooftops. The silence that followed didn't last long. Suddenly, elven swordsmen sprung from the shadows of the ruined buildings and launched desperate attacks. They aimed for cheap shots, catching a handful of men off guard and claiming a few lives with quick, ruthless strikes.

However, the dwarves and humans quickly regained control. The elven warriors, though fearless, were outmatched by the disciplined force. The humans' shields and dwarves' axes made short work of the ambushers. One by one, the elven swordsmen fell, their final resistance snuffed out in the dust and rubble of the ruined street.

The battle was over. The men lowered their shields and caught their breath, exchanging relieved glances. Dwarves and humans alike took a moment to clean their blades and mourn their fallen, their breaths misting in the cool air as they gathered their strength.

"We press on," Tholgar grumbled, wiping the blood from his axe. Cael and his commanders nodded in agreement. They communicated quietly amongst themselves.

With a collective breath, they regrouped and continued their ascent, moving towards the steep steps that wound up the mountain, where the elven stronghold awaited.

"Laerion. Laerion!"

King Zelder wandered into his Royal Council room, looking annoyed and confused at the same time. There was no one sitting at the fancy advisory table, even though there was supposed to be a meeting happening at that moment.

The war had been brutal so far, and now a siege from an unknown source was cutting off the castle's external food supply. The fire giants, who were supposed to be staying in the capital, decided to return home to the south. After the death of their beloved leader, Kragor, they were downbeat and heartbroken, tired from battle and long days of walking.

Deserters were becoming more and more common by the day. But there was one person who wouldn't abandon the Crown, even in times like these. And that person was-

"Laerion, are you here?"

A voice answered the elven King, coming from far above: "I am."

Laerion glanced up, startled. He was outraged to find his chief military advisor sitting on the King's throne. "How dare you?"

"Oh, relax. It's just a chair, Your Majesty. And by the end of the day, it won't even be your chair."

Zeldar went pale at those words. He stammered, then managed to say, "You're supposed to be out there fighting for me!"

The older elf chuckled. He slowly got to his feet and started to descend the steps of the throne. "With what? A few hundred starving men-at-arms? A couple of dozen witches who hold no power unless they're hiding under that bloody golden trapdoor? The fire giants aren't here. The King's Guard is a collection of pretty statues out back. And you, well... you're fine with a sword, Your Majesty, but even I have seen the writing on the wall."

When the pair drew level with one another, Zeldar grabbed Laerion by the lapels of his dress uniform. He spat, "This is treason."

"This is reality, you stupid whelp! We made a play for power instead of peace. We failed. Now, be a man and face the bloody music. Sometimes you win. This time, we lost. Now, offer me a last drink before those thugs bust down those fancy doors."

King Zeldar gave the older elf a little shove and took a step back.

Their heated exchange was interrupted by a deafening crash at the castle gates, shaking the very walls around them.

At that moment, the gravity of their situation dawned on young Zelder. He realised they had to make a stand. "Grab your sword," he demanded.

With a splintering crash, the great hall's main doors finally gave way. A mix of elite dwarven guards and fast-moving human sappers flooded the room, looking for guards who had long since abandoned their posts. Soon after, the leaders of two island nations walked into the room, led by King Cael, Princess Marcella, and King Tholgar Ironfist. They stared at Zeldar, who was standing next to the golden trapdoor, looking more frantic by the second. He tugged and pleaded for entry.

Cael's voice rang out, cutting through the chaos. "Well, well, well! Look what we have here, men. Elves! but these are actually alive." The room exploded with laughter from both the humans and dwarves.

Zelder's expression shrivelled with anger, rage igniting within him. "Go fuck yourself. We have suffered enough; if you're here to take over, do it; it's yours."

Tholgar turned to King Cael with a huge smile. "Cael, I would like to finish this myself."

Cael nodded in acceptance.

Zelder's weary smile was meant to be disarming. But it did little to stop the dwarven king.

Tholgar walked with a spring in his step towards Zelder whilst slowly delivering words from the heart: “This is for the thousands of innocents killed, this is for all my fallen men, this is for the years of suffering your kind has put onto others. You don’t deserve to breathe the same air as us; you don’t deserve life in this world.”

Tholgar then turned to his men, “Put him on his knees.”

“Yes sir,” they said as they rushed to oblige.

Tholgar took the sword out of Zelder’s scabbard and placed the cold metal tip beside his neck before holding it away. With one swift motion, he cut through the elven king’s neck.

The room fell silent for a moment as Zelder’s head slowly rolled towards Laerion, Whose jaw was on the floor in shock.

Tholdar then aggressively grunted and pointed at Laerion; he was next. Blood bubbled from his lips, and tears ran down his cold, elven cheek as he was stabbed through the heart.

The general of the elven army slid off of his sword, quite dead. He rolled backwards before coming to an abrupt stop at the foot of the throne.

Scowling, Tholgar looked down at the two dead elves, spitting on them in disgust. Then he turned to his men, pumping his fist in the air and letting out an almighty war cry. Everyone joined in—victory at last.

Smiles spread around the room, followed by cheering, hugging, and handshakes.

“Silence!” shouted Tholgar. “Cael, come here.”

Cael looked at Marcella in confusion. He slowly turned to his men, puzzled. Who does Tholgar think he is speaking to the King that way?

“What is it, Tholgar?” King Cael said angrily as he stopped over to him.

“Kneel before your new High King of Eldoria,” demanded King Tholgar Ironfist.

Again, a moment of silence spread around the great elven hall as the men of both sides gasped in shock before King Cael erupted in laughter. He looked in the direction of his men behind him.

“Who does this little shit think he—”

Swoosh.

Blood splattered across the faces of the audience as King Cael’s vision spun; his head snapped out of alignment with his spine as it detached from his body and slowly tumbled down his front onto the floor. He had no more breath to use for words.

He ended up viewing the throne room on its side as his severed head lay atop the cool stone floor. His vision quickly faded, and the reign of the elven empire came to a sudden, brutal end.

"NOOOOOO!" screamed Marcella as she fell to her knees in tears. She was in total shock. The whole room stood, frozen in time, shocked at the events that had just unfolded.

A friendly foe offered a hand of condolence to the young princess's shoulder before she suddenly rose and burst into an electric sprint towards the self-proclaimed 'High King'. Raging with a vengeance, she charged towards the dwarf, screaming with her already bloodied sword raised in front of her, determined to kill.

Tholgar took a steady stance, put his left foot back, and reached with his right arm towards his snug belt. He unclipped his beloved axe from its sheath before tilting it sideways and, with a flick of his thick, hairy wrists, sent the weapon hurtling towards Marcella.

Marcella collapsed to the floor, blood poured from her neck. Her head was already meters away from her body as the two separated with momentum; it slid next to her father's lifeless body.

Before anyone could react, Tholgar signalled his men. The dwarves launched themselves at the humans, axes gleaming in the dim light of the hall.

The humans were taken by surprise—though trained soldiers, they hadn't expected treachery from their supposed allies.

Chaos erupted as the dwarves, smaller but fiercely skilled, cut through the humans with ruthless efficiency. Swords clashed, and the grand hall, which had moments ago echoed only with strained words and beheadings, was filled with the loud sounds of clashing steel. Blood spurted up the walls and flooded the marble stone floors.

The humans tried to fight back, but they were unprepared for the ferocity of the dwarven assault. Dwarven shields deflected sword strikes, and their war hammers crushed the bones of the human soldiers who attempted to defend themselves. One by one, the humans fell, overwhelmed by the sheer brutality of the attack.

With the humans dead, the dwarves stood triumphant, the last resistance in the hall wiped out. The grand hall of Ardenviel had become a tomb, not for elves alone, but for the human soldiers who had once been allies. Tholgar raised his bloodied axe into the air, and his dwarven warriors let out a triumphant roar, their voices echoing through the shattered city. The alliance was no more, and now the dwarves stood alone, ready to claim what remained of Ardenviel and crush anyone who stood in their way.

Chapter Seventeen

"The humans cannot know. Not now. Not ever. If they find out we're the ones who struck down their king and princess, everything we want will crumble to dust." demanded Tholgar as he paced behind the head of the table before he continued, "The bodies of their king and princess were consumed in the chaos of battle—burned beyond recognition by fire. It was a tragedy of war and nothing more. Their ashes mingled with the soil they fought to protect. That is what they will be told; that is what will be written in the books of history."

Tholgars previous council had been ripped apart by war. New faces, ones he didn't recognise filled the seats along the long table, a sight that didn't please him, especially with not one daring to speak first.

"Well? Have none of you got anything to say?"

Still, nobody dared say a word.

"You useless bunch of wet leaves who appointed you idiots, not one of you has the balls to speak; either that or you're all missing your fucking tongues!"

"Well, you see, my king, not many people know what happened precisely; different stories have already spread among the troops and surviving citizens." said a nervous dwarf.

"Thank you, finally! Well, what stories are they then? Don't be shy; I want to know," King Tholgar said calmly as he tried to lure more information out of the trembling dwarf.

"Well, there are too many to tell- I've heard, so many I-"

"Well, tell me at least two then!" demanded Tholgar, his voice now giving way to anger.

"I've heard that you killed them, and I also heard that they were crushed by roc,k" fell out the dwarf's quivering mouth.

"Hmmm, well, let me assure you that as long as there are different stories to tell, and they aren't too similar, the Humans will not be able to truly know what happened. We must let these stories thrive. I will do my part when I address the people of this city, but for now, let the tales continue, encourage them if you must, make some up, and just do your duties! This concludes the meeting; get out of my sight"!

With the King's ranting done, the room cleared in seconds.

"Brothers!" Tholgar called out, his voice carrying across the streets, "King Cael and Princess Marcella... have sadly fallen. The elves laid a trap for us all, and unfortunately, they were the first in; they were beyond brave. The Elves slaughtered them in cold blood, desperate to hold onto their throne, but I avenged them with my own hands. Please hear me, people of Blackheavan; their sacrifice was too great. Let it be known that the humans and dwarves fought side by side until the bitter end, and their bravery will never be forgotten."

The human soldiers, though confused and shaken, largely believed Tholgar's version of events. After all, he had a reputation as a fierce but honourable leader, and few could fathom the depths of his betrayal.

"Together, we will rebuild this magnificent city; we will send ships for our loved ones. Skell will once again be a united nation. Well, make good of the lands; we will never go without; we will restore Ardenviel to its grand self, from Torreldane woods to Kilton, the lands will regrow, and the beauty of Skell will be around us once more. This is the future we want. This is the future we need, and this is the future of our children."

The sound of applause erupted from the thousands of men surrounding King Tholgar as he stood there proud of his well-crafted speech.

"And now," Tholgar concluded, "we stand on the cusp of a new era. A time of peace, prosperity, and unity! Let this city, Ardenviel, be the shining beacon where humans, dwarves, orks, and all others may live as one!"

The crowd erupted in cheers. Tholgar smiled, his plan working perfectly. With the humans now firmly rooted in the city, they would be far easier to control—and should any dissent arise, they would find themselves surrounded by dwarven warriors loyal only to him. The future of Ardenviel was secure, and under Tholgar's rule, a new chapter had begun—one forged in blood and deceit, with none the wiser.

Chapter Eighteen

Tholgar Ironfist, now the uncontested High King, sought to bring a new order to Skell; he wasted no time establishing rule over the land. With a keen sense of both justice and pragmatism, he set about reshaping the landscape of power. Their first decree was to free the prisoners on the infamous island, a place long feared for its grim reputation. Those imprisoned, many for minor offences or political dissent, were granted a second chance at life under the new rulers. This act of mercy won the Dwarves' support from the common folk, marking the beginning of a reign that balanced strength with diplomacy. The trip was mostly successful; at least three-quarters of the 300 soldiers who set out to retrieve the prisoners made it back with around 200 prisoners; they lost one boat due to being attacked by the Stomatosuchus. This was already accounted for, though, in the planning; it was the first ship to approach the island and was used as a decoy; the commander of the fleet knew this, just the poor sods who were sailing that particular boat didn't. Istana was now once again completely deserted; everyone was either dead trying to get on the boats or were actually on the boats, no in between.

The Dwarves also dealt swiftly with the remnants of Queen Elaena's loyalist forces. Any giants still loyal to her were banished from the mainland, their ties to the fallen queen severed forever. Huge boats, built with Dwarven precision and designed for peaceful journeys, ferried these exiled giants to distant lands. Tranquillity marked this sombre exodus, but it caused a deep rift in the giant community. Some giants accepted the new crown, choosing peace and allegiance to the Dwarves, whilst others remained fiercely loyal to Elaena, bitterly leaving Skell with resentment in their hearts.

Next, King Tholgar and his newly formed council turned to matters of resettlement. Tholgar extended an invitation of peace and unity to the various races that inhabited Skell and its surrounding islands. The humans, still reeling from the chaos of war, accepted the offer eagerly, surrendering their weapons, titles, and land in exchange for the promise of a new start. This allowed Blackheaven, once a proud human stronghold, to be peacefully reabsorbed into the mainland of Skell under Dwarven rule. Unbeknownst to the humans, however, was the secret betrayal that had taken place within the castle walls. King Tholgar had not only secured a military victory but had quietly manoeuvred behind the scenes, shifting alliances and plotting to solidify their control over Skell, whilst the humans remained blissfully unaware.

The snowpeople, hardy and proud, refused the offer. The harsh, frozen North was their home, and they had no interest in abandoning it for the warmth of the Southern lands, even under new rule. They remained independent, standing alone as the last race, not under the Dwarves' reign.

The Orks, fierce and unruly as ever, were divided. Gron Ironfang rejected the Dwarves' offer outright, unwilling to give up his power and dominance over their island. However, Tholgar's offer of peace and resettlement tempted many Orks who had grown weary of constant battle and conflict. Around 500 ork families chose to leave their homeland, travelling across the sea to start new lives in the capital city of Skell. It was a momentous shift in ork culture, with many torn between their desire for power and the appeal of peace.

Beneath the mountain, hidden from the turmoil of the surface world, the elves of the underworld carried on as if untouched by the war that had toppled their once-mighty rule. Their vast underground city, made of gold, diamond, and precious stones, continued to flourish, illuminated by the soft glow of enchanted crystals embedded in the walls. This hidden Kingdom was a marvel of elven craftsmanship and magic, with bridges spanning deep chasms, intricate arches lining the walkways, and towers that reached up towards the surface. The Elves, despite their defeat above ground, thrived in this secret sanctuary, their society intact and flourishing in secret.

The elves carried on with their traditions, continuing to study Elaenas magic and perfect their arts.

The defeat of their armies on the surface unbeknown to them, almost irrelevant, for as long as their underground Kingdom stood, they felt secure in their isolation. They knew that the enemy, whoever it was, had no knowledge of their true strength or whereabouts.

Above them, the Dwarves were baffled. After securing their victory, they explored the elven fortress atop the mountain, confident they had taken full control. But there was one mystery that confounded them—an ornate golden hatch that lay in the centre of the grand hall. The hatch raised slightly from the marble floor, was covered in runes and intricate carvings that no Dwarven scholar could decipher. Despite their best efforts, they could not find a way to open it. Their best blacksmiths and engineers worked tirelessly, trying everything from brute force to carefully applied techniques of their craft. They brought their finest tools—hammers forged in the deep forges of Hammerdeep, chisels made of the hardest metals—but nothing could even scratch the surface of the hatch.

Days turned into weeks, and still, the golden hatch resisted all attempts to unlock its secrets. The Dwarves, known for their stubbornness and their mastery of engineering, were utterly confounded. Their frustration grew as they realised that, despite their dominance over the surface, something unknown still lay beyond their grasp. They had no idea what was beneath the hatch, and the mystery began to gnaw at their resolve. Some believed it held treasures beyond imagination, whilst others whispered of dangerous magic or ancient curses locked away by the Elves.

As time passed, unease settled over the Dwarves. The unknown had always made them uncomfortable, and the golden hatch became a symbol of that fear. Even their bravest warriors hesitated to linger near it, and rumours began to spread among the Dwarven ranks. What if the hatch contained something far worse than treasure? What if it was a doorway to a power they couldn't control?

Fearful of what might lie beneath and unable to open it, the Dwarves made a difficult decision—they would seal the hatch forever. Using their finest metals, they welded it shut, ensuring that nothing from below could ever emerge. The weld was reinforced with layers of steel, and guards were placed to watch over it, though no one dared linger too long near the site. They felt a sense of relief but also a lingering dread. They had shut away the unknown, but it still weighed heavily on their minds.

Unbeknownst to them, the elves below continued their lives, undisturbed by the Dwarves' actions. The hatch had never been a doorway meant for the surface-dwellers, and it remained a secret only the elves understood. Safe in their subterranean haven, the elves watched as the world above forgot about them, thriving in their hidden realm, waiting for the day they might return to the surface in strength once more. The Dwarves ruled Skell, but the true power still lay, silent and unseen, deep beneath their feet.

Thus, King Tholgar Ironfirst secured the rule of his race over Skell, their power cemented by careful strategy, mercy towards the defeated, and force where needed. The island became a place of uneasy peace, with humans, Orks, and giants settling into new lives under Dwarven dominion.

On the first day of the new year, a few months after King Igor Ironfist claimed the throne, he gave a public speech in the heart of Ardinvel; as thousands gathered, his deep and husky voice echoed through the narrow streets of the city. He imposed a new set of 10 laws that were once unwritten rules. These rules were designed to secure their reign, ensure loyalty, and prevent rebellion from any faction, including humans, Orks, and other species. These rules filled the locals with anger.

King Tholgar began listing the laws off one by one:

1. Disarmament of Non-Dwarven Factions: All non-Dwarven factions—humans, Orks, and any other races—were required to surrender their weapons upon entering any Dwarven-controlled territory. Failure to comply would result in immediate exile or imprisonment.
2. Tribute to the Crown: A yearly tribute in gold, precious stones, or resources was demanded from all settlements and regions, including human lands, as a symbol of submission to the

Dwarven Crown. This tribute helped fuel the Dwarven economy and military.

3. Prohibition of Giant Alliances: Any giant still loyal to Queen Elaena or suspected of harbouring sympathies towards the old elven rule was to be banished from Dwarven territories. Giants loyal to the Dwarven Crown were allowed to stay but under close supervision.
4. Banned elven Magic and Lore: All elven magic, artefacts, and teachings were outlawed. Anyone found practising or studying elven magic was severely punished, and all relics from the elven Kingdom were confiscated or destroyed.
5. Mandatory Dwarven Overseers: In every major city, village, or territory under Dwarven control, a Dwarven overseer was installed to enforce the laws, collect tributes, and report any suspicious activities directly to the Dwarven King.
6. Cultural Suppression of Former Elven Dominions: Former Elven cities, statues, and cultural landmarks were either repurposed or destroyed. The Dwarves aimed to erase the legacy of elven rule, and speaking too highly of the elves was considered treasonous.
7. Resettlement of Loyalists: Any human, Ork, or giant who pledged unwavering loyalty to the Dwarven Crown was resettled in the capital or nearby lands, provided they surrendered their titles, lands, and weapons. They were given lower social status but allowed to live in relative peace.
8. The Ban on Secret Societies and Gatherings: All secret gatherings, societies, or meetings between

different factions were strictly forbidden. The Dwarves feared conspiracies or revolts and made it illegal to organise without Dwarven permission.

9. Mining and Resource Exploitation Rights: Only Dwarves were permitted to mine precious resources like gold, silver, and gems. Any non-Dwarven attempts at mining or extracting resources were harshly punished. The Dwarves maintained a tight grip on Skell's wealth, ensuring that no other race could challenge their economic superiority.
10. Sightings of foreigners: Any sightings of people or beasts not recognised as citizens of the mainland were to be reported to the local authorities immediately.

These rules helped the Dwarves maintain order and suppress any potential challenges to their reign. However, they also sowed seeds of resentment, particularly among the humans and Orks, who found themselves increasingly frustrated under the new rulers of Skell. Many of them felt as though they had been betrayed and lied to by the King, who promised them a better life if they resettled from their home islands.

Chapter Nineteen

The capital of Ardinvel had grown under King Tholgar Ironfist's rule, bustling with the trade and industry of Skell's new era. Despite the strict rules imposed by the Dwarves, there was one thing they couldn't control: the wild imaginations of young boys and girls. And among the most adventurous of them all was an 11-year-old boy named Finnian Vennpok.

Finnian, or "Finn" to his friends, had always been the curious sort. His small stature and scrappy build didn't stop him from trying to keep up with his older brother, who had fought in the skirmishes before the dwarves fully conquered Skell. Though too young to remember much of the elves, Finn's family had spoken of them in hushed tones, recounting the legends of Queen Elaena Fikshire and her mysterious powers. They spoke of the river where she had gained her strength, a place long lost to time, where stars once touched the water and left their magic behind.

Finn, with his boundless energy and determination, couldn't resist a good adventure. Neither could his two best friends, Kara Grasbrook, a wiry girl with a knack for climbing, and Jory Windward, a slightly pudgy boy with an infectious laugh and a love for food. The three of them had been adventuring together since they could walk. They explored the hidden corners of Ardinvel, sneaking past the dwarven guards when they could and imagining themselves as heroes from the tales of old.

On a crisp autumn day, with the leaves just starting to turn gold, the trio hatched their most daring plan yet: they were going to find Redmarch River, the very place Queen Elaena had supposedly gained her legendary powers.

"I bet if we swim in the water, we'll get powers just like Elaena," Kara teased as they gathered in their usual spot outside the city gates. "We'll come back and make the dwarves run away, just like she did to the elves."

"Maybe I'll be able to fly," Jory said, grinning as he mimicked, flapping his arms like wings. "Or maybe turn invisible, sneak into the bakery, and eat all the pies!"

Finn grinned, though his thoughts were more serious. Unlike his friends, he'd always believed there was something real behind the legends. His older brother had once told him that the magic of Skell hadn't disappeared; it had only gone into hiding. And the river... well, that was a place where magic could still be found if you were brave enough to seek it. Many people had visited the river in the hope of finding some more magic, but they were never successful; people in Skell believed the dwarves had taken all the magic from the river and hidden it in the mountain; of course, these were just made up stories.

“Come on,” Finn urged. “Let’s stop talking about it and go before the overseers catch us. The River won’t find itself.”

With backpacks filled with bread, cheese, and a few apples Jory had swiped from his mother’s pantry, the trio set off. The outskirts of Ardinvel were dangerous, especially for small children, but that never stopped them. They had slipped past the dwarven patrols hundreds of times before, ducking through the abandoned fields and into the dense forests beyond.

After hours and hours of walking and dodging patrols, the forest revealed itself. The trees here were ancient, towering oaks and willows, their branches reaching high into the sky like gnarled fingers. The ground beneath them was soft with moss and leaves, and the only sound was the rustling of the wind through the trees.

“This way,” Finn said confidently, pointing towards the southwest. “My brother once said the river runs near the old oak trees. We follow them, and we’ll find it.”

Kara and Jory exchanged glances, but neither doubted Finn’s sense of direction. He had led them on enough adventures to trust his instincts, even when they seemed a little far-fetched.

As they walked, their laughter filled the quiet forest. They joked about what powers they would get from the river, mocking each other in good jest. Kara insisted she'd become the fastest runner in all of Skell, whilst Jory continued to dream of his pie-thieving invisibility.

"I think I'll be able to talk to animals," Finn said suddenly, surprising even himself. "Imagine that... Speaking to wolves, dragites, even the Giants. They'd help us fight back against the dwarves."

"You know the giants speak our tongue anyway, right?" Kara said, giggling. "Why not something fun? Like...I don't know, turning into a fish or something?"

Finn just smiled and replied, "If I were a fish, Jory would find me and eat me."

Jokingly, Jory responded," I'd look for you and make sure it was you; I'd be able to tell, you know."

As the trio carried on walking, Finn started to get lost in his thoughts. He couldn't shake the feeling that this adventure was different, that something real awaited them at the end of their journey. Hours later, just as the sun began to sink low in the sky, they found it: the Redmarch River.

It was more beautiful than any of them could have imagined. The water shimmered with a soft, silvery light even though the sun hadn't yet set. It flowed gently over smooth stones, creating small ripples that sparkled like starlight. The riverbank was lined with moss-covered rocks, and the air around them seemed to hum with a strange energy, as if the very ground was alive with magic.

“We found it,” Jory whispered in awe, dropping his pack and running to the edge of the river. “We actually found it.”

Kara laughed, already kicking off her shoes. “I’m going in! Maybe I’ll turn into a mermaid!”

Finn stood at the edge, watching as his friends splashed into the water. They laughed and played, tossing water at each other and shouting about how they could feel the magic running through their veins. Jory even scooped up a handful of water and pretended to drink it, his eyes wide with mock surprise as he declared, “I can feel it! I’m changing! Watch out!”

Kara doubled over in laughter, splashing him with more water.

Finn couldn’t help but laugh, too, but something in the back of his mind kept him on edge. He watched the river closely, noticing how the water seemed to swirl in strange patterns, almost as if it were alive. And then, out of the corner of his eye, he saw it.

Something glowing.

"Hey, what's that?" Finn asked, stepping out of the water and pointing downstream. A faint purple glow shone from beneath the surface of the river, not too far away.

"What's what?" Kara asked, splashing Jory again. But Finn was already running. He was desperate to get their first, just in case.

He sprinted down the riverbank, his heart pounding in his chest. As he got closer, the glow grew stronger, pulsing with a soft, almost otherworldly light. It was beautiful, unlike anything he had ever seen.

There, caught between two rocks at the edge of the river, was a stone. It was small, no bigger than his fist, but it glowed with a powerful violet light, casting strange shadows over the river.

Without thinking, Finn leapt into the water face first with his arms stretched out and picked it up.

The moment his fingers touched the stone, a shock of energy shot through his body. His vision blurred, and he felt the world spin around him. For a moment, he thought he might drop the stone, but something—some invisible force—kept his grip tight.

He felt the power surge through him, like a bolt of lightning coursing through his veins. It was overwhelming, filling him with a warmth and strength he had never known before. The stories were true. The river, the magic... it was all real.

"Finn?" Kara's voice broke through the haze. She and Jory had caught up to him, their faces full of concern. "Finn, what's happening?"

"I...I don't know," Finn whispered, staring at the glowing stone in his hand. He could feel the power inside him shifting and growing. It was as if the stone had unlocked something deep within him, something ancient and powerful. The purple light faded from the stone, but the energy inside Finn remained. He could feel it humming in his chest, a constant pulse of power waiting to be used. His friends stared at him in awe, unsure of what to say. Finn's eyes slowly turned purple, and his hair turned white.

"I think... I think I have her powers," he said softly. "Just like Queen Elaena."

"Finn, look at your eyes. They are purple," Jory said, his eyes wide with excitement. "Your hair is white."

Kara was silent, stunned, and couldn't believe the stories were true. She walked over slowly to Finn and slowly combed her slender hands through his thick white hair. Then, quietly, she mumbled, "You can save us from the dwarves."

"No," Finn said quickly, his voice firm. "We can't do that. If the dwarves find out... they'll send me to Istana. They'll come after all of us, and they will send you two as well, including my family!"

Kara nodded, her expression serious. "He's right. The Dwarves don't want anyone having power but them. If they knew about this...about you—"

"We'd be dead," Finn finished.

For a long moment, they stood in silence by the river, the weight of the discovery settling over them like a heavy cloak. They had joked about gaining powers like Elaena, but now that it had happened, the reality was far more terrifying.

"We have to keep this a secret," Finn said at last. "No one can know. Not even our families."

Kara and Jory both looked at each other before Kara turned to him and said, "Your hair is white, and your eyes are purple; everyone knows the story, and your parents will notice straight away. You can't go home."

The realisation hit Finn like a bird flying into a window —he couldn't go home, not like this, not with his hair turned snow-white and his eyes glowing. If anyone saw him, they'd know. The dwarves had spent years trying to find any source of magic, or anyone who showed signs of it—especially the kind tied to Skell's legendary past—would be taken immediately. Finn would be sent to Istana, the hot prison island from which no one ever escaped.

Panic began to rise in his chest, but Kara's voice cut through it.

"We'll figure it out," she said firmly. Her face, normally lighthearted and playful, was serious now. "But first, we need to hide you."

Jory, still trying to process the transformation, muttered, "But where? People will be looking for him. His parents, the overseers...everyone will wonder where he's gone."

Kara thought for a moment; then her eyes lit up with a spark of an idea. "The barn! The old one, a few miles out. No one's used it in years, and it's far enough from the city that the Dwarves won't be patrolling there."

Finn closed his eyes and looked up to the sky in pure dread, remembering the place she spoke of. It was a rickety old structure on a farm long abandoned, hidden in the overgrown fields outside Ardinvel. The roof leaked, and half the walls were covered in ivy and riddled with every spider, bug, and insect known to mankind, but it was secluded. Safe.

"I could stay there," Finn said, his voice quiet but resolute. "At least for a while. Until we figure out what to do."

Jory nodded, though his usual smile was nowhere to be seen. "We'll bring you food. Every day. And maybe some clothes... something to cover you up so no one sees your hair and eyes."

Kara's expression brightened slightly. "A hooded cloak! We could find one that fits you. Maybe from my uncle's old supplies." Her uncle, a tailor in the city, always had extra fabric lying around, and he wouldn't miss one cloak.

Finn sighed in relief. It wasn't much of a plan, but it was something. His friends had always been there for him, and even now, when everything had changed, they were still by his side.

"We need to make sure people believe you ran off and didn't come back," Finn said, his eyes narrowing as he thought. "If anyone finds out you've been helping me... you'll be in just as much danger as I am."

Jory winced at the thought, but he agreed. "We could say you got lost. Maybe you went deeper into the wilds and never came back."

Kara nodded slowly. "It's not far from the truth. We can say you got separated from us after we crossed the river."

They all stood in silence for a moment, the weight of what they were about to do pressing down on them. It felt wrong to lie, especially to their families, but the alternative—telling the truth—would put all of them in danger.

"We'll do it," Finn said at last. "I'll hide in the barn, and you tell everyone I ran off."

Jory and Kara exchanged one last look, then nodded in unison.

By the time they reached the outskirts of the forest, the sun had dipped below the horizon, casting long shadows across the fields. The barn was just as Finn remembered—weathered and leaning slightly to one side, with tall grasses growing up around it like nature itself was trying to hide it from view. "We'll come every day," Kara said as they led Finn towards the entrance. "Bring food, clothes, and news of what's happening in the city." "And if anything changes—if the dwarves start searching for you—we'll figure something else out," Jory added.

Finn felt a surge of gratitude towards his friends. Even though he was the one with strange, new powers, they were just as much a part of this as he was. They were risking everything to protect him.

They pushed open the creaky wooden door and stepped inside. Dust filled the air, and the faint smell of hay lingered in the corners. In the fading light, Finn could make out old tools scattered around, forgotten long ago by the farmers who once worked the land.

"This'll work," Finn said quietly, already scouting out a small corner where he could sleep. He didn't need much, just a place to lay low until they figured out what to do next. Kara rummaged through her pack and pulled out a thick blanket. "You can sleep on this for now. We'll bring more tomorrow." Jory handed him some of the bread and cheese they'd packed earlier. "Eat something. You'll need your strength if... well, you know."

Finn accepted the food, though he didn't feel hungry. The weight of the day's events had drained him in a way he couldn't explain. As he sat down, wrapping the blanket around himself, he noticed his hands trembling slightly. The stone's magic was still humming within him, a quiet reminder that his life had irrevocably changed. "You guys should go before it gets too dark," Finn said, glancing towards the barn door. "The longer you're gone, the more suspicious it'll look."

Kara nodded, her face troubled. "Just stay hidden, okay? We'll be back at first light." Jory gave him a weak smile. "Try not to blow anything up with those powers of yours before we get back." Finn chuckled, though it was more out of nerves than humour. "Yeah, I'll try not to, but I can't promise anything."

As they left, the door creaked shut behind them, leaving Finn alone in the dim light of the barn. He leaned back against the cold stone wall, staring up at the rafters. His mind raced with thoughts of what had happened at the river, of the strange powers he now possessed. He had always dreamed of having magic, of being like the heroes in the old stories, but now that it was real, the burden felt heavier than he'd ever imagined.

What would he do with this power? Could he even control it? What were his powers? And more importantly, how long could he hide before the dwarves—or someone worse—found out?

Finn knew that one day he could change the lives of those suffering under the strict dwarven King, but he was still young. He knew that he had a long while to become a hero; right now, he just needed to focus on surviving.

THE END

General Toric retreating after the defeat to the Fire giants

The Elven Underworld

Orkish Giant War Boar

Dwarven Giant War Elephant

Kragor - Leader of the Fire Giants

The Golden Bunker

A sketch of Queen Elaena Firkshire

A sketch of a Dragite

A sketch of High Priestess Ylvana

Character Index

The High King Draegon – Original King of Eldoria

The Prince of Eldoria – Alarik, son of Draegon

Elaena Firkshire – The first wielder of magic in Eldorian history, also known as Elaena the Punisher.

Braegon Fikshire – Father of Elaena, leader of the Elven revolution, also known as Braegon the Banisher.

High King Zelder Fikshire – Son and successor of Braegon. The younger stepbrother of Elaena.

General Laerion – Elven General

Elandril – The Royal Council's senior diplomat

Nioma – Council magical advisor

Khorgar Ironfist – Father of Tholgar

King Tholgar Ironfist – King of Dwarves

Kozna Duhnmar – Advisor of Tholgar

Baldric Endholl – Advisor and friend of Tholgar

Brokk StoneBeard – Dwarven warrior

High Priestess Ylvana – Queen of the Snowpeople

General Toric – General of Ylvana's army

Gron Ironfang – Cheiften and King of the Orks

Ork Chaplin of Fire – Controls and trains the dragites

Raggok – Second ork in command

Wout – Orkish Warrior

Kragor – Leader of the Fire Giants

King Cael Emberfall – King of Humans

Princess Marcella Emberfall – Daughter of Cael

Thrarxis – Sea serpent

Finnian Vennpok – Child one

Kara Grasbrook – Child two

Jory Windward – Child three

World Index

Eldoria - The Continent where Skell and the other islands are situated.

Skell - The mainland.

Ardenviel - Capital city of Skell.

Torreldane Woods - Large woodland area near the east coast of Skell.

Haleinde - Small village near Torreldane woods.

The Mines - Large quarrying and mining facility where most of the minerals are found on the west coast of Skell.

Montoise - The most westerly city of Skell, cold and wet.

Rivendale - The northernmost city in Skell and the second largest city on the land.

Kilton - A small and forgotten city in the middle of nowhere.

Seacry – Seacry is a large town and is an extremely important fishing location. 80% of the fish brought in is caught here.

Selthor shores – A long stretch of coastline on the east side of Skell. The beaches are hidden behind miles of forest and mountains.

Heavans keep – The castle of Ardenviel.

Mount Morvem – Mountain in Ardenviel.

Jotungard – The Snowpeople's Island.

Hammerdeep- The Dwarven Island.

Grimstone – Mountain on Hammerdeep.

Gruk'Thor - The Ork's Island.

Gorthak – The Great Orkish City.

Blackhaven – The Humans Island.

Istana – The Island of Prisoners.

Mount Harkoth is the largest volcano in all the land, located to the south of Skell.

Redmarch River – This River is where the magical stone was found.

www.ingramcontent.com/pod-product-compliance
Lightning Source LLC
Chambersburg PA
CBHW041746010726
47507CB00008B/296

9781836151487